Ghost of a Chance:
Love in Little Tree 4.25

A Common Elements Novella

Love in
LITTLE TREE

Megan Kelly

Thanks to Cora Lee for organizing the
Common Elements Romance Project; and my
gratitude especially to Lynn Cahoon, who
read this story and laughed (at the right places)
as I took a step into the paranormal;

and as always,
With Love to my husband,
for reasons he well knows.

Copyright © Megan Kelly 2019
ISBN: 978-0997894431

CHAPTER ONE

PAUL TORRES clamped his back teeth together to mask his irritation and summoned a fake smile for whoever might be watching him. With his luck, somebody probably was.

This gig working the lamest haunted house in the history of ... well, history, hadn't been his idea. His brother, Mike, had "saved" him by arranging this joke of a community service job. If tortured, Paul would admit he'd appreciated it at the time. Being nearly twenty-one, he could have faced more serious consequences for vandalism.

Not that he'd been guilty. Exactly.

But he'd been with the guys who'd done it, so guilt by association and all that, which he understood, even if he didn't think it fair. Plus, he hadn't stopped the guys from breaking the window or peeing on the walls outside the bakery. And he'd been drinking. Not smoking pot or doing any harder drugs, but drinking underage earned him yet another black mark in his brother's book.

Now here he stood, taking tickets and managing the line going through Little Tree, Montana's sorry excuse for entertainment. It beat the wheat maze east of town, which—thank you, God—he didn't have to work. The younger kids seemed to like it, but they didn't know any better. This town didn't even have a movie theater.

Since moving here the year before, he'd relied on his new friends for excitement. Breaking the window of the bakery—in the alley, in back—hadn't been his idea of fun, but his friend (whose name he wouldn't reveal) had been high and just turned twenty-one. So Paul took the fall to save [redacted] from more trouble.

A glance at his cell phone reassured him his shift would end soon. He had to usher in this one last group of seven, consisting of two little kids and a dad, and a group of four kids about his age, then he could close up and get out of here.

Paul had been keeping an eye on the foursome, made up of three girls and a guy. He'd been especially eyeing one of the girls, the brunette with the pretty smile and better laugh. As Paul let in up to nine people at a time, he'd watched the four of them advance. Relief had filled his chest when he saw the lone guy sling his arm around one of the blonde girls and pull her close. It looked like a headlock to Paul, but if the girl didn't complain, he wouldn't get involved. Just note to himself not to date a girl he had to strangle to make her stay close. If he'd ever yanked on a horse that way, his brother would have had his hide—if the danged animal didn't bite him already. And maybe even then.

"Last group," Paul called.

"Hey, man." The guy wearing an Avengers T-shirt edged his way to Paul and dropped his voice, like they hung out together. Which would never happen. Paul just got a bad vibe off him. He carried himself more like Loki than Captain America.

"How 'bout you let this family go in and then me and my friends can go on our own?" The guy shot a jovial elbow toward Paul, barely grazing his forearm. He leaned on the temporary stand holding the rope barring entry, acting all casual-like, but with a hard look to his eyes.

Paul recognized the type: the class bully who charmed the adults and intimidated the other kids.

The guy gave a stiff smile. "You know. The girls get all scared and I'm the only guy around they can hang on to. You get me?"

Paul got him. Easily. It didn't take a genius because this guy was just that transparent. "Sorry, man. You seven are in the last group together."

The other guy's eyes narrowed but he kept the smile in place. "I really just want some alone time with my girl. Maybe you could send her two friends with this family and then just her and me could go through. Alone. What do you say?"

Paul flicked a glance at the pretty brunette standing with the two blondes. He could sympathize with wanting time alone with a girl in a dark place. The three girls were whispering and glancing toward Paul and the Captain-wannabe. "I say if your girl wanted to be alone with you, she wouldn't have invited her two friends along."

"Screw you." The guy pushed away. "Loser."

Shrugging, Paul checked the timer again then gave his spiel to the seven outside. Rules came first while they were listening, though that boyfriend guy would need watching. He seemed like the type to knock over a few things "accidentally" and blame poor workmanship for their destruction.

Once the rules were taken care of, Paul set up the story of the haunted house for the two little kids, who he guessed were about six and seven. Good thing the "haunted" part induced more jumps than screams.

The so-called attraction had only opened that night, and already he'd given the speech enough he didn't have to check his notes. He wished the cute girl didn't have to hear him since he'd been instructed to dramatize where he could. Still, he'd never see her again. Little Tree was so small he knew everyone, and he'd have heard from his friends about a pretty girl moving to town. She'd leave tonight thinking he was just some volunteer with nothing better to do, getting into this lame story.

"This house wasn't always haunted," he started the tale.

"Some house," the boyfriend jeered.

"True," Paul continued with a nod to the kids. "It's a shack now, but once upon a time" — the boyfriend groaned at the classic story starter— "a gold miner lived here."

Well, *here* in the sense that he'd been on this land, according to local legend. The old shack had been added on to and repaired for years. This place, he'd been told, represented more of the 1930s than the 1870s, but some of the wooden boards might date back that far. Still, the location was authentic, and 1930 sounded pretty old to Paul.

He continued. "The miner had dug and dug, and panned and panned, over on what's now the western border of Montana."

The little girl shot up her hand. "Is that near Yellowstone National Park? Because that's where we're going once our tire's fixed. The garage was closed when we got here."

The boy added, "Mom said she needed a bottle and a bath before she got back into the car."

"Okay, okay," the dad cut in with a chuckle. "No need to air all our laundry."

"What laundry?" the kids asked.

An idea popped into Paul's head. It wasn't mentioned in his notes, but these kids would never know the difference. Still, he didn't want to lie to a child. He leaned forward as though sharing a secret. "Did you ever wonder if the yellow stone from the name of the Park refers to gold?"

Paul paused as the girl formed an "O" with her mouth and eyes. He immediately felt bad. What if that wasn't true? Crap. Now he'd have to look it up on the Internet so he wouldn't accidentally mislead another kid tomorrow. He straightened and went back to his memorized script. "Because the miner worked hard, he ended up with a huge fortune in gold."

The boyfriend muttered "yeah right" but the two kids edged closer, faces interested. The girlfriend poked the guy in the ribs and shushed him.

"The miner's name was Beezer. The other

miners working near him had been Confederate soldiers, fighting for the South in the Civil War. As a Union man, Beezer didn't trust them, so he planned to leave as soon as he struck it big. But he did make one friend, another miner named Andy who came from the great plains of Kansas. Legend has it Andy couldn't find gold in a jewelry store, but he could play a harmonica, which made him fine company for Beezer. Some people claim they've heard the lonely whine of harmonica music out here on chilly windswept nights."

Both kids' eyes went wide. Paul ignored the boyfriend's snort of disgust. The brown-haired girl smiled, encouraging Paul to continue, and his heartbeat sped up.

"Once Beezer found enough gold nuggets to be considered very, very rich," Paul went on, "he gathered his fortune and planned to go back East where he used to live. He and Andy lugged the bags of Beezer's gold all the way across Montana."

Paul stopped to think of his notes. Because *of course* Little Tree couldn't have a scary haunted house—they had to have an educational one. He swallowed a sigh as he began the shtick about history.

"If you started walking tomorrow, without stopping to sleep or eat, it would take about three days to travel from the western border to here. But back then, Beezer and Andy had to stop to fish or hunt for food and to find water. They had to take care of their mules, to feed and protect them. Every night before they could sleep, they had to build a fire to ward off animals, and they spent all day hiding from Natives and other miners who might be following them."

Paul stopped to let that sink in before he continued. "Despite all their efforts, they only made it as far east as this cabin before Beezer got too sick to go on. He died right here of a terrible fever. Or..." Dramatic pause required before lowering his voice. "Maybe he was murdered for his fortune."

The boyfriend grunted, almost ruining the kids' oohs and aahs. The girlfriend's elbow crashed into the jerk's ribs again. Paul hid a grin.

He liked her. Spark in a girl could be fun. Did the brunette have spark?

Paul checked his timer. The earlier group should be all the way through and everything reset by the other volunteers. He hadn't heard the signal yet, so he went on. "Now remember, this is an old place, standing here even before Beezer moved in, so please don't touch anything." He gave the hard-eye to the jerk. "Besides the possibility of breaking something that doesn't belong to you" —he turned back to the kids— "we can't be sure you won't take some home germs. And I'm not talking about gold fever."

The father laughed. "Any chance of gold *dust*?"

Paul chuckled. Maybe he could incorporate that into tomorrow's talk. Make it more fun for the poor parents who had to accompany their kids. "Sorry, I already checked. No pay dirt, just the regular kind, but we've got plenty of that."

"Shoot," the dad said. "We sure could have used a speck of gold to pay for this side trip."

Nodding, Paul said, "I hear that. But Clem is

a good guy. He won't jack up your cost just 'cause you're from out of town."

The man's eyes widened. "You know the garage owner? Well, I guess you would."

The boyfriend's laugh was full of insult and Paul stiffened, staring at the dad. *Did he say that because I'm Hispanic?* Just because Paul wanted to be a mechanic didn't mean this guy could be rude about it.

"It's a really small town, isn't it?" the dad said. "I bet you know everyone."

Paul relaxed as the other man's meaning became clear. He nodded, since he did pretty much know everybody after being here for a year. "The best place to eat is The Diner. Best place to buy a horse is from my brother."

"Best place to *ride* a horse," the pretty brunette piped up, "is at my dad's place."

Paul pivoted toward her. "What? Where's that?"

"Come *on,*" the little boy whined. "Isn't it our turn yet?"

Paul tore his gaze from her. "Oh. Yeah. Sure." He moved the rope to let them in. "Sorry."

The jerk pushed past with his girlfriend, almost bumping Paul.

"Sorry," the third girl said. "He's an idiot, but she loves him."

The brunette stopped. She stood so close she had to tilt her head back to look at him. He'd bet she stood only four inches or so shorter than him, making her around five seven.

"Yeah," she said in a sweet voice, "we're really sorry. The *three of us* planned to go out *alone*," she yelled the word, "but Randy got all pouty."

"No problem." Paul walked with her toward the wooden slats that made up the porch. A single light pole lit the area and illuminated the parking lot. "What did you say about your dad having a place to ride horses?"

Her smile lit her light brown eyes. "We bought the dude ranch south of town."

"What dude ranch?"

"The Schmitt ranch. The Davis ranch now." She gave a little self-conscious wave. "Hi. I'm Mariah Davis."

"Paul Torres," he replied as they reached the

group. "Is that Mariah like the singer?"

"Like the wind." She grimaced. "Long story involving my mom."

"Hey, *Paul*," Randy the jerk said with a sneer, "can we get this show started?"

The kids' dad gave Randy a steely-eyed glare. "I'd like for my children to enjoy this. Are you going to help make that possible?"

Randy slumped back, visibly cowed, and gave a shrug. "Sure, man. Whatever."

Paul unlatched the front door and shook his head at the kids, putting on a grim expression. "Be safe in there. Good luck."

Both kids grinned at his theatrics.

The third girl walked past him with a slight smile. The boyfriend stopped. Paul braced himself, knowing the guy would have to redeem some street cred after the older man embarrassed him.

"Aren't you going to wish *us* luck?" Randy said in a tough voice.

"Absolutely." Paul widened his eyes at the girlfriend and nodded toward the jerk. "Good luck."

The girls giggled. Randy stiffened and Paul tensed, almost wishing the bully would throw a punch. He'd really like to deck the guy.

"What the—"

"Oh come *on*." The girlfriend pulled at Randy's arm. "Give it a rest." They went past with the jerk only muttering an obscenity Paul didn't bother trying to hear.

"Sorry again," Mariah said, trailing the others.

Paul stepped inside behind her and closed the door, sealing the room in pale green light and murky shadows. He pressed a switch under a table. The timer should activate the fake lightning storm just as the kids reached the third space, where a zombie-like miner endlessly panned for gold. Timing was everything in the haunted house biz.

When the two other girls tiptoed forward, Randy stepped back without looking and bumped Mariah. She dropped the little wallet she carried, which burst open. He mumbled an apology to her, but Paul saw the fist he'd formed. He'd probably planned to hit Paul when the girlfriend moved ahead. Randy's foot encountered something on the floor which he bent and handed to Mariah before shuffling off. The gesture counted for something at least.

Paul knelt and helped Mariah gather her stuff. A lip gloss rolled past him and he dug under the spiderweb-covered opening that resembled a clothes closet but hid a panel of electronics.

"I can get this if you have to keep up with the group," she said. "This clutch is my mom's from the '70s. Vintage is cool, but mom said the clasp pops open like Henry the Eighth's shirt buttons after a banquet."

Paul laughed until he made out her frown in the dim light.

"Although, now that I've said that," she continued, "I wonder if they had shirt buttons back then. Hmm. Probably though, right? Made of bone or something?"

He stared at her, having never considered when buttons were invented. Who even cared? They were pretty common nowadays.

"Coming, Mariah?" the third friend called.

Mariah patted the floor for stray items then rose from her collecting and shrugged an apology to Paul. "I don't want to stick her with them. We're having a pretty miserable time with Randy along."

Did she mean she would have stayed with Paul if that third girl didn't need her? He liked the idea. "Sure. I wouldn't leave a friend with him either."

She glanced around the floor, dark with shadows, and then walked into the next room.

He let her wander ahead, smiling as the kids and girls shrieked and laughed as the surprises jumped out at them. The old shack had been enlarged and divided into a maze. Each turn held the possibility of a ghost or zombie.

Paul preferred the enclosed area past the fourth room since it contained the only air conditioning vent, and he appreciated a break from the heat of the enclosed area, full of warm electronics. October might be bone cold outside, but everyone had on coats or jackets, and the shack suffered from lack of air and too many bodies in the small, man-made spaces.

The chill from the a/c vent preceded Beezer's ghost popping out, which everyone expected because of the temperature change. They didn't expect a second surprise, a cold hand behind whoever was trailing the group—or a third surprise, the drip of a sticky red liquid a few steps farther on. The fake blood didn't touch anyone unless that person reached over the walkway pretty far. Which he'd told them not to do, so a day wearing a stain of red food dye might teach them to pay attention next time.

Just as the kids and father passed the miner, the lightning storm blinded the group. Right on time. Paul smiled as the kids yelped. Volunteers had put this place together long before he'd been roped into working it, but he kind of wished he'd been here for the start. He'd have liked to see the timing and electronics synced. He could have helped with setting up some of it since he was good with motors.

His brother hated that Paul wanted to be a mechanic. Paul agreed to take one class from the community college to see if another subject struck his interest. Unfortunately (in Mike's opinion), with Mike starting up the horse ranch, they didn't have money to spare. Fortunately (in Paul's opinion), Mike agreed to Paul taking a class online, which saved room and board in Billings or the gas and time of a commute.

Paul followed the group through the maze of rooms, already thinking of the steps for closing the place down for the night. He had a checklist which he'd scan when he finished to make sure he didn't miss anything, and he'd pocket the keys since the place wasn't real secure.

Mariah and her friends giggled and gasped, marking their visit as a success.

When the "adventure" ended, they stood out back where ropes tied to posts led the attendees back to the parking lot. The dad and kids thanked Paul for the entertainment. He waved them goodnight, waiting for Mariah's group. Hoping she'd come over and say something, like her phone number so he could text her. But she merely waved and got dragged toward the parking area.

He should have known he didn't have a ghost of a chance with a girl like her. He said goodnight to the two guys who'd jumped out at guests and worked the electronics that weren't on timers. Alone again, Paul checked from the back room going forward on the first sweep. He'd do a second walk-through from front to back and lock up as he went before he shut down the generator.

A creak made him freeze in place, hand halfway toward a broom. Had the jerk boyfriend returned to settle some imagined score? Tense, keeping his hand near the broom handle he now considered a weapon, Paul waited but heard nothing. Seconds ticked past before he exhaled on a chuckle. His first night and he'd let the "haunted" shack get to him. That didn't bode well for the next few weeks here.

Then he heard the front door open.

CHAPTER TWO

MARIAH JUMPED when the dark shadow in the room shifted. "Oh." She laughed. "Sorry, you scared me. I mean, I knew you were still in here, but I didn't see you."

Paul stepped forward from where his dark hair, skin, and clothes had blended in with the room. "Hi."

Nerves took control of her stomach—he was just that cute. She'd gone to school with lots of different personality types in Chicago, but no one had lit her insides the way Paul did. Gathering her wits, she gestured behind her to the door. "I wasn't sure whether to knock. You know... Who answers the door at a haunted house? I didn't want to chance it."

He chuckled. A car horn blew two short

blasts outside.

"Anyway, I lost my keys. They must have dropped out of my mom's clutch."

"That's not good."

Was it wishful thinking on her part that his tone sounded like he meant the opposite? She held up her phone to show the flashlight glow from the back. "I should have turned this on the first time but I didn't think of it. And I wouldn't have wanted to ruin the mood anyway." *Mood?* Jeez. That sounded more intimate than she'd intended. "I mean, for those kids. The haunted mood."

Hopefully it was too dark for him to see her roll her eyes at herself. She hadn't had trouble talking to a guy ... ever. They were just like hairy, muscular girls.

"I have something better than a flashlight," he said. "Give me a sec."

While he went to the corner closet, she tried to pull herself together. He was about as much of a girl as Adam Rodriguez, her favorite actor on "Criminal Minds." Paul's voice reminded her of an actor in that movie her mom had watched last week, *The Mask of Zorro*. He had the silky tones of the young Antonio Banderas when he'd tried to charm his way out of trouble. And that barely-there accent made her knees weak. Basically, he was hotter than chili peppers, and her mouth tingled to kiss him.

A lightbulb flipped on near Mariah and Paul stepped out of the area that turned out not to be a closet but some kind of electronics board. She nodded her thanks and checked the floor. Not seeing her keys, she felt guilty for being glad. The lost keys kept Paul from going home. Selfishly, she couldn't be sorry. She wanted to spend more time with him.

The car horn blew a long sound like a train nearing a railroad crossing.

She groaned. "Sorry. Randy's an idiot."

"Not your fault." Paul gave her a sideways glance she couldn't interpret. He cleared his throat. "If you have to go, maybe you should give me your phone number. I mean, you know, in case I find your keys later."

A laugh bubbled inside her and she swallowed it back. *Thank God*, he was interested in her too. "Why don't I give you my phone number anyway?"

His grin made her heart race. "We should swap numbers."

Mariah handed him her cell phone, and after he tapped in his digits, she called and his phone vibrated. She spelled out her name for him to save in his Contacts. "Now you'll have to think of a reason to call me. Because" —she pointed to the next room where the brighter bulb dispelled the shadows— "my keys are right there."

Paul turned. "Oh."

Her keys, probably kicked by Randy, stuck out beneath a display of tin plates lining the wall. Paul retrieved them for her while she checked a text.

"Hmm," she said. "It says, 'He's such a—' Um, well, there's a lot of cussing." She glanced at Paul. "It's not exactly news that Randy's useless." Her phone dinged. "Oh, wait. His girlfriend, Caity, says 'sorry.' Hmm. I wonder about which thing."

She pocketed her phone, more interested in the guy in front of her than vague messages. "So.

You'll call me?"

"Sure."

"No, really. I don't want to be waiting—"

Her ringtone played "My Kind of Town."

"Sorry." She pulled her phone from her jeans. "This might be important. They never call."

Caller ID read Paul Torres. She grinned. "I wonder which Paul Torres this is. Maybe I should take a picture of you to attach to your contact info."

His eyebrows rose. "So you don't confuse me with all the other Paul Torreses in your phone?"

She tried a flirty smile, hoping she didn't look foolish. "I'll let you take a pic of me."

"Deal." The word shot from him. "Let me turn on more lights in here."

"Let's get Beezer in the picture."

They posed together in front of the zombie miner and Mariah shot a selfie of them. "That's a memorable picture of our chaperone." *And of the night we met.* But that would sound silly. Still, she had a feeling she'd want to remember this.

She sent him the photo then dragged her feet

toward the exit. "Well, nice to meet you."

Paul hurried past her and held open the door.

She peered into the darkness. One pickup truck sat in the parking area.

Her friends had left her.

Ordinarily, she'd be ticked off. Instead she turned to Paul, tamping down nerves and delight. "Well, darn. Any chance you could give me a ride home?"

Paul couldn't suppress a quick grin. "No problem."

Yeah, right. No problem, unlike breathing. No problem, unlike keeping his heart from pounding out of his chest. "Let me close up."

He'd planned to move away from her for a few seconds, hoping to get a break from the feelings that overpowered him when she stood nearby. Instead Mariah followed him around the room. As he shut off the lights he'd turned on, the rooms turned pitch black, and the intimate atmosphere almost overwhelmed him. He could sweep the floors before they opened tomorrow night. No way would he do clean up now. He knew better ways to spend time with her, and he didn't want Mariah to think of him as a janitor.

Would she expect him to make a move? Nothing ventured and all that, but he didn't want to lose whatever chance he had with her. Still, here they stood, in the dark, alone. He'd be loco not to take advantage of this opportunity Fate had provided.

He stuck out his hand. "Maybe you should hold my hand. So you don't get lost."

After a pause, she said, "It's a pretty small space."

God, he was stupid. He stood this close to a nice girl who seemed interested and he had to push his luck. To push her away.

A soft hand slid into his, startling him worse than any ghost.

"But I'd hate to bump into anything." Mariah smiled. "I've been warned against touching the props."

With her hand in his, he felt like he could leap ten feet high. Instead he nodded and moved to the next area, praying he didn't stumble in the dark.

Such a simple thing, holding hands. Like in that Mellencamp song his sister Anita always played. Holding Mariah's hand felt like everything, or at least as much as he was going to ask for tonight. No guy could get lucky twice. Well, three times if he counted meeting her. Four, if he counted her friends' desertion.

Mariah waited while Paul locked up and then shut down the generator out back. He turned on his flashlight app and led her along the path to the parking lot. The two of them could have been the only people left on Earth. His ancient truck door whined as he held it open for her, making him wince. A good mechanic's vehicle shouldn't have creaks, dents, or rust. The truck had all three. But the engine purred as he started her up.

"How long have you lived here?" he asked. "I haven't seen you around."

"We've been busy moving in. Didn't you know the Schmitts sold their ranch?"

"Sure." Paul shrugged. "But you said 'dude ranch' and no one ever thought of it as anything that fancy."

"Well, it'll be a dude ranch soon." She tipped her head toward the open window and her long dark hair blew in the chill breeze the truck created.

"You can roll up the window if you want. I leave them open as long as I can in the Fall. By next week, we'll probably be sealed in for the next seven months."

"It's okay. I like riding with the windows down."

"Why move here?" Paul couldn't imagine choosing this place. When Mike followed Grace to Little Tree, he'd dragged along Paul and their sister Anita.

"It's different from Chicago. My dad wanted quiet."

Paul grunted. "Well, this is the right place for that."

"And Mom sensed this town. So here we are."

"Sensed it?"

"Hovered her hand over a map of the United States, then over one of Montana, and boom, narrowed it down to Little Tree." Mariah studied him for a beat, obviously waiting for his reaction.

He shrugged. "I'm glad you wound up here."

She blew out a breath on a laugh. "Okay then."

"What?"

"You passed. Mom's a little bit psychic. I don't tell a lot of people, and I never have until I get to know them better."

His chest puffed up with pride, threatening to choke him. "But you told me."

"Yeah, it's weird. I just... I don't know. Wanted to see what you'd say."

While he should be ticked at being tested, her worrying about his response told him something about her past experience with people accepting her mom's abilities. Or not. Did he believe in the so-called psychic realm? He wasn't sure, but it'd be nice to believe his parents watched over him from heaven.

"What else does your mom do, other than sense where to move?"

"Séances. Card readings. Love potions."

He darted a glance at her, only to find Mariah biting back a smile. "Very funny."

"She's not a witch. She's just got some talents."

"And you? Did you inherit any of those talents?" Like, would she notice how their speed had dropped to a near crawl so he could spend more time with her?

Mariah eyed him, the green dashboard light lending her an other-worldly glow. She crossed her arms over her chest. "Why?"

Oops. He'd stepped past a line he hadn't even seen. His younger sister, Anita, did the crossed arm thing when feeling pushed or ticked off. Time to lessen the tension. "Just wondering if you could have teleported home. Wiggled your nose or blinked your eyes, and *poof*."

Her silence made him cringe. That ghost of a chance he'd almost had with her had just vanished like fog in the sun. He kept his gaze on the road ahead, feeling his way only as far as the lights allowed. Unfortunately, he didn't have high beams he could use to navigate this conversation with Mariah, and he was making a mess of it.

Then she burst out laughing. "Is the TV reception so slow here you're only just now getting shows from the '60s?"

Phew. "I like the old sitcoms." His parents had watched reruns to improve their English. People talked slower and clearer back then, and the jokes made it easy to grasp meaning. "The newer ghost hunting shows are interesting too."

She grunted. "Most are just bad lighting and garbled sound effects."

Time to bring the subject back to earth. "Why did your dad choose to open a dude ranch?"

"Well." She blew out the word on a breath that indicated this would be a long story. "Dad had a" —she put up air quote fingers— "heart incident. Don't say it was a heart attack around him, though. The doctors strongly advised that he retire from his stressful job in Chicago finance. I mean, he sat at a desk, but whatever. Turns out thinking hard can give you a heart attack."

Paul heard the worry under her words. "I try to avoid it for just that reason."

"No thinking?"

"Not as often as I should."

"Ah, you prefer action."

Her teasing made him shift in his seat. "That sounds better than I act first and think later. I'm sorry about your dad's heart problems."

"He reacted to the news *without* thinking, if you ask me. The doctor says retire, so, boom, Dad's like, 'we have to leave Chicago.' Then Mom picks this place. If I wasn't going to Billings next semester, I'd go nuts here long term."

Billings? That community college idea sounded better and better.

"No offense," Mariah said, "but it's *really* quiet in Little Tree. I've been here a week and if I hadn't bumped into Courtney at the library, I wouldn't know anyone our age lived here."

She must have taken his silence as offense. Time to distance himself from the town so she wouldn't think he was boring too. "Yeah, I just moved here last year and it took some getting used to. There's no movie theater, no fast food joint to hang out at. Not being in school anymore makes it harder to meet people. And everyone leaves as soon as they graduate or can afford to go."

Mariah turned sideways to face him. "Where did you live before?"

"Longmont, Colorado. North of Denver."

"Why did you move here? Got a witch in your family who sensed it?"

Paul laughed at the idea. "Worse. A pushy brother and a new sister-in-law who's from the LT. I mean, she's great. She's a painter, so a totally different vibe from what my family's used to. We're pretty norm—uh, dull."

"Good save."

"How is your mom going to like it here? There aren't any covens that I know of."

"That you know of," Mariah emphasized. "But Mom's not wiccan."

"You said there's a story with her and your name. Will you tell me?"

Mariah sighed. "It was storming when she learned she was pregnant. She says I brought the wind, but I think my name was inevitable because her name is Tess—well, Teresa, and Dad's is Joe."

Still waiting for the bridge that connected these thoughts, he prompted, "And?"

She laughed. "There's an old song with my name, 'They Call the Wind Maria,' but spelled without the 'H.' It's from a musical no one's ever heard of called 'Paint Your Wagon.'"

"You're right. Never heard of it."

"No one our age has, so I don't get teased much. Don't worry about us being weird. Mom's a little unconventional, but she's also a librarian, so she can be pretty dull too sometimes. I got my love of research from her."

"You like research?" He couldn't imagine anything worse than being trapped inside all day with his nose in a book. "What do you plan to study at Billings?"

She sighed. "Still undecided."

Somehow, Paul didn't think so. That sigh sounded more like "let's not get into this again" rather than "I have no idea." He recognized the undertones since he had the same conversation with Mike. A lot.

He pulled into the long driveway, searching for the right words to ask her out on a date. She wasn't like the girls he usually talked to. "Almost there. The Schmitt place." He waved a hand at the house in the distance like a tour guide, unable to stop himself from being an idiot around her. "Safe and sound."

"The Davis place."

"Just so you know," he said as he navigated a pothole, "people are going to call this the Schmitt place for the next fifty years."

Her chin lifted. "Then we'll just have to make such a good impression that no one will remember it belonging to anyone else, nice as they might have been."

"Yeah, um, that's not the way things work here. It's not an insult to your family. It's like... My sister-in-law is known as 'the doc's daughter,' even though she's grown up and really popular in the art world and married now."

"That's cool. Are they planning to make you an uncle?"

"Been there, done that. My older sister has kids."

"I'd love to be an auntie, but I'm an only child, so I'll have to hope my future husband has siblings."

"I'm one of seven kids."

Ah dammit. He really couldn't stop himself from sounding like an ass.

Mariah giggled while Paul jammed the stick shift into Park and doused the lights. He didn't want her to see his embarrassment. "Okay, out you go."

She laughed harder. "Was that a proposal?"

"Nice meeting you. Bye now." He looked out his side window, cooling his cheeks. God, he was such a loser. But in a way, her laughter made it better than awkward silence would have been. He still wished he could disappear into thin air right about now.

"I wasn't expecting you to put yourself forward as marriage material just yet. I mean, not before our first date."

He gave her a look, probably wasted in the dark truck cab. "You just pull up the handle on the door there and push outward."

"I'm only joking."

"I know." He jumped out and grasped her hand to pull her across the seat behind him, making sure she had her footing before letting go. "I'll call you, okay?"

"Oh." She sounded disappointed. "Right. Sure."

"I will."

She nodded. "It's just... Aren't you going to kiss me?"

Back on firmer ground himself, Paul echoed her earlier comment. "Not before our first date."

"So when will that be?"

"Soon, I hope."

Mariah smiled. "Tomorrow?"

"Do you want to come out to the ranch for a ride? I'll probably have some open time right after lunch."

"Oh." She cleared her throat. "I don't really ride."

His jaw dropped in surprise. He waved a hand toward the dilapidated stables. "But...your dude ranch?"

"Well, I mean, I've been on a horse before. Once."

Paul crossed his arms, trying to look disapproving but holding in laughter. She looked miserable and defiant and hopeful. Did she think he'd withdraw the offer to ride? Couldn't she see how much he already liked her? "Once, huh? Where?"

"A friend's birthday party. You know, where they bring a pony on a rope." She drew a circle in the air. "And the owner guy walks you around."

"I have no idea what you're talking about." He did, of course. He'd seen it at the fair. But to call that *riding* made him cringe. "How old were you?"

"Seven. And in case you're trying to ask, I'm nineteen. I took a gap year while my dad was sick."

Paul nodded, relieved she wasn't a minor. He could get into enough trouble without that complication.

But jeez. Not to be on a horse for more than ten years? What was *wrong* with city people? Unless… "Was it traumatic or something?"

"No. The poor old thing barely moved."

He blew out a breath. "Okay then. We'll get you back in the saddle and you'll love it."

"Do you have a sweet, cautious horse that doesn't mind a new rider?"

He pictured the abused horses Mike

rehabilitated and the wild broncs as yet untrained. Too long of an explanation. "We have a couple of well-trained horses. You'll be in good hands. Trust me."

"Oh, I do." She rose on tiptoes and brushed his cheek with her lips before running inside.

Paul watched her go, a huge smile on his face. She was trouble waiting to happen.

He laughed, looking forward to it.

CHAPTER THREE

THE NEXT DAY, Paul watched Mariah's face as she first viewed the ranch. It wasn't much, but it was way closer to habitable than her folks' place. She twisted in the seat to look at everything.

"Cool sign."

His chest swelled with pride. "My sister-in-law, Grace, painted it."

"I love it. The horses look so happy."

He laughed. "That's exactly what she was aiming for."

If Paul's luck held, Mike should be out in the far corral working with the two wild horses he'd just acquired, and Anita and Grace had driven to Billings to shop for clothes and pick up art supplies for Grace. The family bought a lot through mail order, but Grace informed him and

Mike yesterday that "sometimes girls just have to be in a store." Mike's expression conveyed the same bewilderment Paul had felt. Having them gone on an all-day Saturday shopping spree worked out well for Paul's plans.

Knowing they'd be absent had inspired this ride today. He'd taken a chance on Mike meeting Mariah, but his brother trusted him with the horses and wouldn't make him look bad. The two girls though... They'd have asked Mariah all sorts of questions, and God knew what they'd have told Mariah about him.

He introduced her to a six-year-old white mare named Sugar, of all things. Worse abuse than the name had been applied to Sugar by her owner. Mike had almost used the whip on the guy when he saw her condition. "Sugar is as sweet as her name. She prefers female riders, and once she hears your soft voice, she'll give you a gentle ride."

"Should I pet her?"

Paul bit the inside of his cheek. The city girl didn't know a horse from a dog. He took Mariah's hand, which gave him the chance to hold it, and guided her palm to Sugar's neck. He watched the horse's ears and body language for tension.

"I thought you'd have pink eyes," Mariah said to Sugar in the sing-song tone Paul's older sister used on her babies.

"Thank God she didn't. Her previous owner considered her bad luck from the moment she was born." Paul didn't add that every setback the man suffered turned into lash marks on the horse's flesh.

"Because she's white?"

He nodded.

"That's silly," Mariah cooed. "You're so pretty and sweet. I bet you've lived up to your name."

Sugar acted sweet now, after working with Mike, but the horse had come to them wild-eyed with a tendency to kick and bite.

After Mariah delivered a few more pats and coos, Paul drew her hand away. "That's enough for now. She doesn't need contact like puppies do."

Nodding, Mariah stepped back and bumped into him. He felt the surge of lust through his body. "Ohh!"

She'd felt it too?

But when he glanced away from Mariah's dark hair brushing against his chest, he had to smile. Sugar was head-butting Mariah's arm. "Guess she wants you to touch her again." He and the horse had that in common.

"She trusts me." Mariah looked over her shoulder at him, her smile turned all mushy.

"That doesn't mean you don't have to keep an eye on her."

"Right."

He didn't believe her for a second and pulled her backward. The girl was a goner for the horse.

Paul saddled up Sugar and another rehabilitated chestnut named Tiger—honestly, what was wrong with people?—and helped Mariah into the saddle. Adjusting her stirrups, he sent up a prayer for her to have a good ride.

They set out on a slow walk to give Mariah confidence. The horses got along, which was why he'd chosen Tiger, the most docile and laziest horse in the stable. If Tiger had been a little more predictable, he'd have put Mariah on the gelding. But every once in a while, Tiger swished his tail and tore off in a run so fast few riders could stay in the saddle. Mike was working on this tendency and trying to figure out what spooked him. Until then, Tiger couldn't be trusted.

"C'mon, Sugar," Paul called as the horse once again stopped to graze. Mariah wouldn't use her heels on the mare and she tried not to put any weight on the horse. Her thighs would probably scream when she dismounted. She shook the reins tentatively against Sugar's neck, but so lightly the horse probably didn't feel even a tap.

He clicked his tongue and Sugar complied.

The third time this happened, Mariah giggled. "Which of us are you clicking at?"

He raised one eyebrow at her. "Are you going to fall in line if I" —he made the clicking noise— "at you?"

"Doubtful."

"I didn't think so." He winked and held out his hand. "Come on, sugar."

She and the horse moved closer.

After clearing her throat, Mariah asked, "Is the haunted shack really haunted?"

He shrugged. "Depends on if you believe in ghosts. I don't know why anyone would stick around that place or why spirits get stuck here, if they do. His friend Andy was supposed to take the gold to Beezer's kid. Maybe Beezer's waiting for news. Or a doctor. Or revenge."

"Do you think he was killed for his gold or was that just added for the kids?"

"He died and his gold was never found. Makes a good story either way. But locals said he died of a fever. Whether from placer mining or mercury fumes or something he picked up from the, uh, paid women in camp, no one knows." Paul needed to change the subject; prostitutes didn't fit the tone of the day. "I know someone we could ask who was probably alive back then."

"Oh, come on. No one's alive who's that old."

"Seriously," Paul said, not at all seriously. "He's like a relative."

She shook her head. "How can someone be 'like' a relative?"

"He's my brother's wife's sister's husband's uncle."

Mariah gaped. "Does that even count as

family?"

"*La familia es muy importante* in my culture," he said slowly in Spanish 101.

She rode in silence for a moment while Paul bit the inside of his cheek, trying to keep his expression neutral.

"I can't tell if you're making fun of me or not."

A chuckle broke through his pretense. "Crusty probably is that old. Whether him being my sister-in-law's sister's uncle-in-law makes him related to me is debatable. Most days I wouldn't claim him, but sometimes he's pretty funny."

"I think your ghost in the shack wants to know if his friend double-crossed him," Mariah said. "And whether his child got his fortune."

"He wants to know or you do?"

She raised her chin. "We both do. So, has anyone researched it?"

"I'm sure someone has. Being near a fort, Miles City probably had a newspaper back then and covered this area. They might have covered deaths."

"It would be easier if we had something other than a nickname."

"We have a rumor." That got her attention. "I was told the history committee vetoed including it in the haunted shack talk because it's not confirmed. Beezer's last name might have been Raines."

Mariah's jaw dropped. As her hands went slack on the reins, Sugar stopped walking to eat, and Tiger followed suit.

"Why didn't you mention this before?"

"I told you, it's not verified, so it wasn't allowed. There's not a Raines family in town." Paul paused, not liking the gleam in her eye. "Why?"

"Oh, nothing," she said too casually. "Just wondering if there are old articles about Mr. Raines on the Internet."

He gave an internal groan. Looked like he'd be doing some research in the near future. But since he'd be with Mariah, he figured he could tolerate a day of cyber-boredom.

"Okay," he said on a sigh, "we'll go do some research. Come on, sugar."

She gave him the hard-eye and he stifled a chuckle.

After Paul took care of the horses, he drove Mariah to her house. She liked watching him with the animals. He displayed strength and a kindness with them that he probably didn't know showed. He'd been patient with her lack of riding skills, and she'd enjoyed the ride more than she remembered from the past. Of course the company was also twenty times better today. She'd need a hot bath later to relax her aching leg muscles, but she didn't regret a minute of it.

She hadn't met any of Paul's family, but he didn't escape meeting hers. Thankfully, it was just Mom, which could be interesting. Mariah couldn't wait to see them interact. Paul hadn't been freaked out by stories of Mom's talents, but he also didn't believe in them. Yet.

Mariah glanced around the kitchen, glad Mom had started dinner, freeing up Mariah from the prep work. Sliced mushrooms and celery waited on the cutting board. She lifted the lid on the pot and inhaled. Stew bubbled. "Hmm," she said. "Needs more eye of newt."

Her mom turned and swatted her playfully on the backside. Mariah whimpered. After a day of riding, she couldn't afford the consequences of teasing her mother.

"Mrs. Davis." Paul held out a hand in greeting, looking confident. Mariah suspected his curiosity about her mom being a witch had overcome any nerves he might have had about meeting her parents.

"So nice to meet you. Please, call me Tess."

Mariah watched her mom's face as they shook hands. The serene blue eyes stayed steady on him. As usual, her mom's thoughts remained a mystery. Was she picking up anything from Paul?

Mom gave one nod in Mariah's direction as the handshake ended.

Mariah exhaled with relief. She didn't have any doubts about Paul, nor would she let her mother's "reading" him sway her. But dating Paul would be a lot easier with Mom's approval, however it was attained.

"Thank you for taking Mariah riding," Mom

said. "She needed the refresher."

"She did well," Paul said, his formal words making him sound ancient. "But as we didn't even trot today, perhaps I should take her out a few more times. For her safety."

Mom laughed. "I knew I'd like you."

Mariah rolled her eyes at their instant bonding. "We're going to do some research in the den." She turned to Paul. "It's the only computer in the entire house set up with internet. The previous owners should have had a cell tower installed on their back acreage. I could have used my cell phone for research, and the tower rent payments might have saved their ranch."

"But if they had, you wouldn't be here," he countered.

"Good point. I guess I can live with dial up for a few more days."

"Anything I can help you with?" Mom asked.

"No. Thanks. We're just starting, but if we get stuck, I'll let you know."

"Nice to meet you," Paul said.

Mariah practically had to drag him away from her mother's radiant smile.

The hall was dark and the den contained a pile of moving boxes. "We're going to paint so we don't want to unpack the books and stuff yet. Maybe we'll get new carpet."

They'd *definitely* take up the worn, mud brown carpet, but she didn't want to be disrespectful of his previous neighbors.

She pulled a hard wooden chair to the desk and gestured for him to use the upholstered rolling chair. Of course he refused. She booted up the machine and waited while the gear icon spun. "Want a drink?"

He narrowed his eyes. "Is it made of leaves and eggs and spider webs?"

If that pertained to witches, she didn't know the reference. "I'm having a Sprite."

His eyes went wide in mock horror. When she caught on, she laughed. "As in, the pop," she said. "Made by Coca-Cola. Not an elf."

"Sounds good, thanks."

Mariah went into the kitchen and filled two glasses with ice. Tension crawled across her shoulders as she waited for her mom to say something. Foam rose and died in the glasses before Mom spoke.

"He's nice."

Mariah faced her with relief. "Is that it?"

"Do you mean did I sense anything when I touched him?"

Mariah nodded, not sure she wanted to know. It felt as though Mom had invaded his privacy somehow. But since Paul didn't believe in her talents, would he even care that Mom had tried to read him?

"He's a nice young man, baby. I like him. And so do you."

Mariah went still. Had Mom sensed something? Mariah didn't even know what her feelings toward Paul were, other than physical attraction. And, eww, she didn't want her picking up on that tidbit. "Why do you say that?"

"The eye of newt joke, right in front of him. It means you told him about me."

Mariah cocked her head. "You don't usually care if I tell people."

"You don't usually test your friends this soon after meeting them. That's telling, and I only have to be a mother to see the significance there."

"I've asked him to keep quiet about your talents."

"Let me get a week in at work first. I'll see how stuffy the library staff is and judge how they'll take the news. Maybe I won't go public here."

"Until there's a lost child or pet."

Mom sniffed. "It wouldn't be neighborly if I didn't help search."

"And your 'luck' at finding lost people, pets or random items is legend."

"What are you two researching?"

"Nothing you'd be interested in." Mariah picked up the glasses and headed for the door. "Just a ghost."

Her mom screeched in excitement behind her, making Mariah laugh. "Not yet, Mom."

"Let me know when you're ready for me to help."

As she set the glasses on the desk, Paul asked, "What was that all about?"

"I told her we're looking for a ghost. She probably wants to reach out with a séance."

"Would that be faster than the Internet?"

"It'll be faster than our computer." She drank some pop, stalling while she thought of ways to prolong their time together. "If we don't find anything here, we could go to the library."

"Whatever you want, sugar."

She raised an eyebrow. "Is that going to be a thing?"

"Oh, look," he said with a little more enthusiasm, "a search engine."

Mariah didn't argue about the endearment, kind of liking it.

They input the information they had. GOLD MINER, BEEZER RAINES, LITTLE TREE MONTANA, 1800s

Neither showed surprise when the search came up with gold mining, gold mine history, and numerous Montana sites. "Should we put in 'fever'?"

Paul shook his head. "What if he died of something else? Doesn't have to be murder, but maybe... I don't know. Whatever was going around back then."

"Syphilis?"

He winced. "Could be. I mean, you can search for 'fever' if you want."

She added both terms. They watched the spin of the icon, then she scanned the link titles and descriptions. "Lots of gross articles I'm not going to click on."

"Good." The ice tinkled in his glass as he gulped down his pop.

Mariah slumped in the chair. "You didn't mention a proper name for the ghost last night on the tour. Does anyone know what 'Beezer' is short for?"

"If they know, they didn't put it in the presentation notes."

She smiled. "Should we ask your relative, the old guy?"

He laughed. "He might actually know. I'll call Grace's sister later and have her ask him."

"In the meantime," Mariah paused and took a breath for courage to ask him out yet *again*, "do you want to go the library and see if they have any old newspapers archived?"

His face fell into lines of what she hoped was genuine disappointment. "I can't. Sorry. I've got chores at the ranch this afternoon, then I have to work at the shack tonight."

When he didn't say more, she nodded. "I understand."

"Could we do it tomorrow? The library's open on Sunday afternoon."

Her relief probably showed, but she didn't care. "Tomorrow."

As she opened the front door to see Paul out, her father stepped in. "Hey, pumpkin. Oh." Dad came to a halt and drew himself straight. "Who's this?"

Mariah froze. Her dad tended to be a little hard on her dates.

Paul extended his hand. "Paul Torres, sir."

"We met last night," she said as they shook hands. "Paul took me riding today."

"Last night, huh?"

"I think I'm going to like riding," she cut in. "More than when I was a kid."

Did he hear that not-so-subtle reminder she'd grown up?

Dad put his hands in his front pants pockets and rocked on his heels. "I take it you live in

Little Tree?"

Either Dad didn't hear her or was ignoring her message.

"My family has a horse rehabilitation ranch west of town."

"And how did you two meet?" Dad turned to Mariah with a sharp look. "I thought that girl you met at the library and her friends picked you up last night."

"Joe," Mom cut in, "give the boy time to answer. Or actually, don't. I believe he's on his way out. But perhaps you could come to dinner tomorrow or later this week?"

"He can't," Mariah rushed in. "He has to work."

That took a little starch out of Dad. "Where do you work?"

"I'm volunteering at the town's haunted shack for the next few weeks."

Mom beamed. "Volunteering? How nice. That benefits the school, right?"

"Yes, ma'am."

"I'm tempted to go." Mom sighed. "But I need to stay away from— Wait, is it really haunted?"

She turned to Mariah. "As in, there's a ghost? Or more than one?"

Mariah sighed. "Yes, Mom, there's *possibly* a ghost, but probably not. But yes, that's who we're trying to learn more about. And no, Paul can't stay tonight or come to dinner this week because of work."

She pushed on a very amused Paul, who fortunately shuffled out the doorway since she wouldn't have been able to move him without his cooperation.

"Nice to meet you both," he called before she shut the door.

The next afternoon, Paul rounded the aisle at the library having found a book on the area's history. Spotting Mariah at a table with a stack of books by her elbow, he had to chuckle. In the time it took him to find one book, she'd acquired half the history section. He sat at the end of the table by her and checked the titles. Gold mining, illnesses of the 1800s, horseback riding for beginners (which made him smile), histories of Montana before and after statehood, baby names (which made him gulp), and how to communicate with ghosts. He tapped the last one and whispered, "Do we need this if we have your mom? You said she does séances."

She glanced at the book then raised one eyebrow. "I'm hoping not to involve her."

"Why? Wouldn't it be quicker to use an expert?"

"I don't want her to be witchy here."

He nodded. "I won't tell anyone."

"Let's try to do our research first then we'll decide. I found some copies" —she gestured to the open file folder in front of her— "of microfilmed newspapers. I wish every newspaper had copies on paper. It'd save my eyesight."

Paul had no experience using a microfilm or microfiche machine but he'd seen them on TV shows when people did genealogy searches. He scanned the room. "I wonder if Mrs. Browning works any days still. She retired, but she does some volunteer stuff here. She'd help us with this research."

"Who's that?"

"She used to be the librarian forever,

according to Grace, my sister-in-law." He leaned closer. "Mrs. Browning is going to be my sister-in-law's stepmom."

"Another person who's nearly a relative?"

"Yep. As it turns out, the town's full of them."

"That's another career I'd like to have, but librarian jobs are few and far between."

"What other jobs are you thinking of?"

"I love history, but that means teaching, which *I* think would be okay, or writing about history, or finding someone who needs a researcher. Maybe a history author. But those are few and far between too."

"Do you want to teach?"

She shrugged. "It'd be okay as a way to immerse myself in history. You probably know all the history of the Old West, but I can't wait to learn more."

Paul didn't know how to answer. He didn't really know more than he'd had to learn in order to pass tests in school, and he'd forgotten most of the facts ten minutes after the final exam. On the other hand, he didn't want her to think he didn't understand her passion. She'd gone riding with him, after all, sharing one of his interests. "I probably don't know as much as I should. Are you going to study education?"

"No. Dad wants me do something that makes a lot of money so I'm financially secure and independent. He'd like me to work in the stock market, like he used to."

Paul grinned. "Well, now that you live in the West, tell him you're going to sell cattle. That's the definition of stock market around here."

She laughed. "Oh, he'd love that. After he saw his cardiologist's bill, he suggested I could be a heart surgeon, but the lack of interaction would drive me nuts. I'd be taking a scalpel to my colleagues within a week."

"Then you probably shouldn't do that."

"No. Probably not."

"Have you told your dad how you feel?"

She looked at him with wide honey-brown eyes. "You don't have a father like mine."

"No father at all, actually, but my oldest brother sets pretty high standards. Like, he wants us to be happy and healthy and not kill our co-workers."

She smiled. "That *is* quite a high bar."

"But," Paul said, "he wants us to be happy most of all. I bet your dad wants that for you too."

"Maybe."

"Does your mom like working in the library?"

"Loves it."

"So follow your dream. Look where your dad's dreams got him—having a heart attack and now shoveling horse manure."

She arched a brow. "If you think my dad is shoveling anything, you didn't pay attention when you met him."

Oh, he'd paid attention all right. Her dad didn't like him. Whether that was something personal or just a dad protecting his daughter from any unknown male, Paul couldn't yet tell. But a wall had gone up in the guy's mind. Now Paul had to decide how long he wanted to bang his head against it. Looking at Mariah, he knew he'd give it a few more knocks. "No, I don't see your father doing anything more strenuous than giving orders."

"He's not that bad."

Paul shrugged.

"Back to our research." Mariah tapped the open book before her on the table. "There's nothing yet about anyone nicknamed Beezer and no Raines who was famous in Montana. I'm doing a scan for Ebenezer as I read. Can you think of any other name that would be shortened to Beezer? It's so odd."

"I figured it was probably Ebenezer too. I could ask Crusty about old names."

"Sure." She pushed the baby name book toward him. "In the meantime, try this."

Ah. Now it made sense. He flipped to the boys' names, starting with B.

Paul lasted fifteen minutes before the urge to move hit him. He fought it, changing positions in the chair, looking up from the book every once in a while to refocus his eyes, and stretching his neck. Working beside Mariah, who smelled like some kind of flower, he forced himself to remain seated.

Maybe it was the book boring him to death. None of the names hinted at a shortened version being Beezer. He'd gone to the last page. Zebadee came closest but was backward of what they needed.

"I'm sorry, sugar," Paul whispered after half an hour. "I need to get home. I have to do some chores before working at the shack tonight. Being Sunday, we're not open as late, so they said to expect the crowd to come early."

She shut her book. "I understand. Let me check out the books that are loanable. We may have to come back to search in the reference books."

He jumped up and carried the stack of books to the counter for her then waited while she chatted to the teenage clerk checking out Mariah's books. Two weeks in the town and Mariah knew the circulation staff. He'd been in Little Tree for a year and didn't even have a library card.

He glanced around, wondering what the library had to offer him. His face went cold when he spotted the jerk from Friday night sauntering toward them, without the calming influence of his girlfriend.

Randy leaned on the counter on the other side of Mariah, way too close. "Hi."

"Oh, hi." She glanced past him. "Where's Caity?"

He shrugged. "Not here."

"Why are you in Little Tree?" Mariah asked.

"Caity said this is where you met Courtney last weekend. I thought you might come back." The toothy smile Randy probably considered charming looked more like a shark with the midnight munchies. "I thought we might get together."

I'm standing right here. Paul narrowed his eyes but Randy didn't take his gaze from Mariah to notice. Paul wanted to yank her away and put her behind him, hidden away from this pri— sleazeball.

"Oh," Mariah said, taking a few steps from the counter, out of the way of other customers, but keeping her voice low. "Is Caity coming by here?"

She was too sweet to read between the lines. It wouldn't occur to her to double-cross her friend, so she didn't understand that Randy planned to do just that.

"No. I mean, but she might. Maybe later."

No, she wouldn't. Randy had no intention of including anyone else. But he didn't balk at insinuating Caity might show up, just to get Mariah alone.

Paul's chest filled with rage. His hands formed fists and he forced them straight. "We'd better get going."

Randy finally looked at him. "Didn't see you there. You leaving?"

"We are." Paul's hand wrapped around her upper arm, staking a claim. He had to resist the urge to tug her away.

She glanced at him with a look he couldn't read, but he could guess at its meaning.

Okay, so the move reeked of being territorial. He had no rights over her, despite the surge of anger in his chest. He just couldn't—wouldn't—see her with this guy. "We better get going."

"Chores," Mariah explained.

Although he'd used the word earlier, now with Randy listening, it sounded like the busy work of a little kid earning his allowance.

"I can run you home," Randy put in.

"No," Paul blurted out.

"No," Mariah said at the same time, though in a still-quiet tone in deference to their surroundings. "I mean, thanks, but that's not necessary. Paul will take me."

The jerk smirked. "But he has chores."

Paul's back teeth locked together so hard he thought the muscle bulge might break his jaw. "I can make time."

Mariah glanced at him with a question on her face. "If it would be bet—"

"No. It wouldn't be."

"Dude," Randy said, "let me help you out. I've been wanting to meet her dad anyway. To ask about a job."

Oh hell no. Paul was so angry he barely noticed Mariah's eyes widen. This jackass working on her dad's property, being around her all the time? Acid boiled in his stomach because Paul knew he couldn't do a thing to prevent that from happening.

"You'd actually be helping me out," Randy said to Mariah, playing on her kindness. "I need the job, and I'm good with horses. I mean, I don't love mucking out stalls, but it's necessary, you know? I do it for my uncle; have every summer since I could hold a shovel. What do you say? We're going in the same direction, to the exact same place."

"Well..."

Paul looked away, not willing to see her give in. Her soft heart would rule.

Her hand touched his arm. "It would save you time."

"Whatever you want to do." But please, he thought, don't choose him.

She shrugged and collected her pile of books. "Then thanks, Randy. I guess you're taking me home."

Mariah's dad burst outside when Randy pulled up in front of the house. His steps slowed when he noticed the car rather than Paul's truck. It would have been comical but Mariah didn't feel like laughing. She'd evaded Randy's hand during the trip, countered his suggestions they get a drink, have some dinner, take a drive, go see his uncle's property, or go to a movie in the nearby town. Her temples pounded with a tension headache and she was in no mood to humor another man, even her dad. First Paul had left her—okay, she'd been a little dim there, not seeing Randy's less-than-noble intentions, but Paul sure hadn't fought very hard. *Whatever you want to do.* Hmph.

She scowled, mostly at herself. Had she expected him to drag her away to his lair like some mythical monster? King Kong maybe? Though, he had staked a claim with that hand on the arm bit. Her skin had tingled, and truth be told, she kind of tingled now remembering it.

Randy's car door opening broke into her thoughts and she pushed at her door as well. He'd already approached her dad. Her first thought was that Paul would have run around to open her door for her. She could operate the latch just fine, thank you, but a guy showing good manners had nothing to do with her ability.

"Dad," she said as she approached, arms loaded with books—another thing Paul would have helped her with. "This is Randy. I don't know his last name. He's Caity's boyfriend. He'd like a job here, so he brought me home from the library to meet you."

Her dad narrowed his eyes at her rudeness. Randy's body had gone stiff, but that could be nerves at meeting a prospective employer.

"I would have brought her home anyway, sir." Randy extended his hand, which Dad shook. "Randy Rogers. You might know my uncle, Burt Rogers. Everyone calls him Buck, like this character from an old sci-fi TV show."

Because of course, she thought sourly, he believed everyone had heard of his family. "We've just moved here, Randy. We don't know that many people in the town, let alone everyone in the county."

"I've heard of him," Dad said, surprising her. "He has a reputation as a tough boss but also for producing good cattle."

Randy beamed. "That's Buck. I've been working for him every summer since I could hold a shovel."

Mariah had to fight to keep her eyes from rolling. He'd found a line he liked and milked it for every situation.

"I'm not really hiring hands yet," Dad said, earning her ever-lasting gratitude. "We're still tearing down and rebuilding. Besides, your uncle counts on you. How do you figure you'll have time to work two places?"

Sweat beads popped out on his skin. Randy stuck his hands in his pockets. "Buck has full-timers who need the work. I would never try to take their jobs. I'm only here for the summer before I head to Bozeman. I've been accepted at Montana State."

He reminded her of a peacock she'd seen at the zoo in Chicago. Strutting. Proud of himself. She couldn't stand it. "I'm going to go put these books down. Thanks for the ride."

"Oh, hey, I'll call you, okay?"

She grunted a response as she walked off.

Fifteen minutes later, her dad came into the kitchen where she helped Mom make dinner. Mariah glanced up from dicing cooked chicken for stir fry. Dad wore a scowl, aimed at her. She waited for him to speak, guessing Randy had caused trouble somehow.

"I've been talking to that boy you brought to meet me. The second one, I mean. Today's. After what he told me, I don't want you seeing that kid."

"What boy?" Mom asked.

"Fine by me," Mariah said. "I have no interest in Randy."

Dad scowled harder and crossed his arms. "I don't mean Randy. I mean that first one. Pablo."

Mariah glared at him. "His name is Paul."

"I thought Randy said his name was Pablo." Dad shook it off. "That's not the point. I don't want you going out with him."

"Why?" *Please don't say because he's Hispanic.* It would break her heart to learn her dad held such a ridiculous prejudice.

"What's this about, Joe?" Mom glanced between the two of them, a furrow between her eyes. "I liked Paul."

"Well then, you've both been fooled. Randy filled me in on his past." He turned to Mariah. "Do you know why he's working at the haunted house?"

She shook her head.

"Community service," Dad crowed with a tone full of I-told-you-so.

Breath caught in her throat, Mariah didn't know what to say. She wanted to defend Paul but she didn't have any details. Community service meant some kind of crime had been committed, didn't it? She just couldn't believe it. Paul held her door open for her and didn't kiss before the first date. He was somebody's brother and somebody's uncle.

"What did he do?" Mom asked for both of them.

Dad shrugged. "Randy didn't say, but you don't get sentenced to community service for walking old ladies across the street."

CHAPTER FOUR

MONDAY FOUND PAUL cranky and tense. Mariah didn't answer her cell phone, making him wonder what happened. Just bad luck getting through to her or had he done something wrong? He replayed their time together and couldn't come up with anything off. Actually, it had all felt so right, to him anyway. Maybe it had something to do with that prick Randy. Paul knew he should have taken her home from the library. Should have said to hell with his chores and his unpaid, forced-volunteer job at the shack. Mariah was twenty times more important. Already.

His biggest fear, the one making his stomach hurt, was that his reputation had caught up to him. He'd never tried to hide his past, but he didn't exactly brag about it on a first date either.

A nice girl like her wouldn't want to go out with someone like him. He wouldn't say he had a drinking problem, but he came home drunk more often than he should. He had an apprenticeship-type job, meaning he barely earned spending money for a date night, let alone made anything to save for college. The garage in town hired him to detail the cars before they went back to their owners. The only positive was watching over the mechanics' shoulders while they worked on vehicles, and doing the occasional oil change or tire rotation. He hung out with friends equally underemployed and a little too wild. Paul didn't want Mariah to know the path he was on, mostly because it led nowhere.

All day he felt at loose ends. Working with the horses usually distracted him, as it reminded him of his parents. Papa had loved horses, having much of the same affinity with them Mike did. Today, though, the work didn't satisfy or calm him.

Mike noticed, of course. He noticed everything having to do with the animals. As they gathered for an early dinner in deference to Paul's job, Paul tried to shake off his mood, or at least hide it.

"You got it bad for that girl," Mike said.

"And fast," seventeen-year-old Anita added with a wicked grin. "Like a virus."

"How long have you known her?" Mike asked. "Two or three days?"

"Isn't that the typical incubation period?" Anita teased.

Paul shot her a sour look.

Grace shook her head as she sat at the table. "Leave him alone. It looks serious."

She'd become one of his best friends as well as family. "Thank you," Paul said.

She turned to Anita. "But don't you get too close. It might be catching."

Anita rolled her eyes. "After growing up with four brothers? I'm totally immune."

Later that evening, Paul half-heartedly gave the haunted shack spiel for the third time since opening. For a school night, they'd had a good crowd, with some repeat customers bringing their kids after checking it out over the weekend.

As though the town of Little Tree would sponsor anything genuinely too scary for children. He gave an internal eye roll, counting down the customers and trying to figure out when they'd decide to shut down. He didn't have the authority to make that decision, but he would sure support either of the two men if they suggested the shack closed early. If it wasn't too late, he'd call Mariah and see if she wanted to...

Do what? There weren't many attractions in this town. Kerr's Grill probably didn't have live music on a Monday. She would have eaten dinner already, but maybe she'd agree to having a pop or a snack. Anything to make her want to spend time with him.

"Is this place really haunted?"

Paul's head snapped up, and he grinned when he spotted Mariah standing by a small girl with yellow pigtails. He glanced at the other people around and recognized one of her friends from the first night. Not Randy's date, but the other one. They'd been standing with their backs to him, the blonde shielding Mariah from his view. "Hi."

"Hi," the girl—what was her name?—said. "This is my sister, Daisy."

He nodded before letting his gaze wander back to Mariah. He hadn't seen or talked to her for a whole day and he'd missed her voice. He'd missed the way her smile lit her honey-colored eyes, and the way she swung her long, straight hair out of her face or pushed it behind her ears without thinking. He'd like to be the one moving it out of her eyes for her and stroking her soft cheek. "Hey, Mariah."

"*Hola.*"

He choked on a laugh.

"So," she continued with a tip of her head to the little girl he guessed to be about six years old, "is it haunted?"

Paul nodded solemnly for Daisy and for the other family standing behind Mariah. "No one can say for sure if you'll meet a ghost, but others say they have. People have heard a lonesome harmonica howling with the wind at a time of night when no one should be out here playing music."

The little girl's eyes went wide and the mom

behind Mariah smiled. Good crowd.

"In a minute, when the people in front of you have come out of the shack—if they do get out, that is" —he hid a smile when Daisy's blue eyes went wider— "you'll get the chance to meet Beezer, the man who owned this place one hundred and forty years ago."

"Is he in there?" the boy with the family asked. He looked to be about ten—and about to pee his pants.

"Maybe, maybe not." The compromise between maintaining the fun aspect of the shack and not scaring the kids didn't reassure this boy. Paul shrugged. "Parents, hold tight to your kids."

Mariah's laugh broke the mood, drawing the young boy's attention. "Who's going to hold my hand?"

Daisy volunteered before Paul had a chance to open his mouth. He couldn't leave the line unattended anyway. "If you're frightened, young lady," he said to Mariah, "you can wait out here with me."

"Come with me and Courtney," Daisy begged.

"I will," Mariah assured her. "This is going to

be fun."

And damned if she didn't go in with her friend and Daisy. He could barely hide his disappointment. When he'd seen her in line, he'd foolishly thought she'd come to see him. That she'd wanted spend time with him. That she'd missed him today too.

As the mom passed, she leaned toward him. "Don't worry about the children. This shack helps them be brave, despite their fears."

"O-kay." He wouldn't have said he *worried* about that.

"The children who went through the shack this weekend came into class today raving about it. I teach third grade, and their talking about the haunted house encouraged the other kids to come. I told my son that I had to come check it out as the teacher so I could recommend it or not."

Paul nodded, not sure what the woman wanted him to say.

"I'm not suggesting you make the talk scary, but don't worry about making it less scary than it is."

"Uh, okay." He was totally confused now.

"Kids have to deal with a lot of things in their lives," she continued, sounding like a shrink on some podcast. "This is an opportunity for them to conquer their fears, overcome them, and have a basis for confidence in trying unknown opportunities in the future."

Paul fell back on the scripted responses. "Thanks for your input, ma'am."

He did his spiel for the group, not shy about dramatizing it tonight. Mariah had heard it and she'd seen him outside of working here. His qualms about her opinion of him had changed from the night before. Now he only hoped she liked him.

Okay, so his concerns hadn't changed that much. At least she waved at him before going inside. He went in and set the lightning storm timer, unable to catch Mariah's attention.

Paul watched the exit while he recited the speech for the next group, in case she snuck out of the shack before the others. Hopefully this would be the last bunch of the evening so he could talk to Mariah. It was a weeknight, after all, and the parents should be concerned about their kids going to school tomorrow.

Paul almost laughed at himself. He sounded like some old person. Even under Mike's eagle eye, he'd managed enough late nights out to brag about to his friends. Of course, he hadn't exactly been a stellar student worrying about his grades.

The beep sounded on his walkie-talkie indicating Mariah's group had exited. He would have to go into the building with this last group when their visit started and hit the timer on the lightning storm effect. Would she leave without talking to him? Wishing he could take out his phone and text her to wait, he spoke to the next group and then let them inside when the double-beep signal came that the rooms were reset.

When they passed into the second room, he stepped out and closed them in.

Mariah waited for him. "Hi."

He smiled. He smiled even wider when he didn't see the other two girls. "Did your friend leave you behind again?"

She glanced around. "Oh, darn. It seems so."

"You'll need a ride home, I guess."

"I left my mom's car at Courtney's. If you could take me there when you're done working, that'd be great. But she lives out off Route 12."

"Not a problem." Could she tell that inside he was jumping around with relief like some kid? He really needed a cooler inner self. "Looks like we'll be done soon. I'll just have to lock up."

"That's okay. I can wait."

"You'll have to, seeing how Courtney left you here." He cocked his head. "You know, you really should meet better friends. People you can rely on." He stepped over and lowered his voice, inviting her closer. "People who would stick around." He bent until their lips almost touched and spoke against her skin. "People who would make sure you were safe."

Mariah drew back. "Uh, yeah. Speaking of that."

He blinked, a little off balance. "Of that what? Sorry, what are we talking about?"

She blew out a deep breath. "My dad heard you weren't really working here as a volunteer but that you have to. That you were sentenced to community service or something."

Dammit. Paul's heart nearly stopped, and he swallowed his panic. If she learned the truth, would he lose her? "It's more like the 'or something.'" While he paused to find words, he realized she'd arranged to be left alone with him despite having heard this. His stomach jolted with twenty different emotions. She trusted him. "I wasn't arrested. It's not like a court-ordered sentence."

She took his hand. "What is it then, Paul?"

Her soft hand and the total faith on her face as she waited for his explanation churned up his gut. He wanted to be worthy of her trust. His past behavior, both here and in Longmont, seemed like some little kid's rebellion. Asinine and pointless. And now potentially destructive.

"I was with some friends who did something stupid. We were drinking, including me. A window got broken and—" Embarrassment burned his face as he thought of them peeing on the walls in the alley. "Some buildings got, uh, marked."

"Tagged, like graffiti?"

"Not exac— Uh, kinda?" No need to gross her

out. "Anyway. The owner of the broken window is on the committee that formed the haunted shack, and he called my brother Mike, and they arranged this punishment off the books. So, no arrest, no court date, no record."

Mariah nodded a little uncertainly. "Why did you break a window?"

He shrugged. "We were drunk. I didn't break the window, but I'm not proud of being part of it. And I'm sorry your dad found out. He's probably not real thrilled you're with me."

She looked away.

The truth seeped into view, drip by drip. His gut went hollow. "Your dad doesn't know we're together. That's why your car is at Courtney's house. So it wouldn't be spotted parked out here. Near me."

She nodded, still not looking at him.

He squeezed her hand. "Thanks for coming. For believing in me enough to ask me about it, even after hearing what you did. And for trusting me enough to send your friend away."

She glanced into his eyes. "Courtney's parents paid for our tickets to bring Daisy. She had to get Daisy home, and I wanted to stay."

The beep signaled that the group would exit now. "I have to stay and close up. You know the drill and how long it takes. But I can get one of the guys to take you to Courtney's if you'd feel better. Or if it would make it easier for you. I know them both. One's married with a baby, and they're both trustworthy."

"I'd rather wait for you."

Relief loosened his shoulders. "Great. Let me tell them to go on home, and then I'll close everything and lock up."

Mariah watched him leave and blew out a breath. That was close. Asking about his sentence had been risky. If she hadn't liked his answer, hadn't trusted him after what he might have admitted, what would she have done? Walked the hundred miles to Courtney's parents' house? On a dark road at night? Until she heard his explanation, it hadn't occurred to her she wouldn't like his answer, that she could ever wind up not trusting him.

How had he earned her confidence so fast?

Living near Chicago, she'd always been cautious. Growing up with a mom with "talents," she'd been slow to open up. But within an hour of meeting Paul, she'd gotten in a car with him, told him about her mom, taken him home with her, and tonight, she had arranged to be stranded with him.

Of course, within moments of meeting him, she'd also wanted to kiss him, so maybe the speedy timing of the rest shouldn't surprise her.

Mariah accompanied him as he closed and locked the shack, and a little thrill ran down her spine when he helped her up into his truck cab, handling her as gently as a china figurine. She felt like a fraud, since she was perfectly capable of scrambling into a truck by herself. Nevertheless, she liked his attention. Liked the way he smiled at her with his sexy mouth. Liked the glint of interest in his dark brown eyes, as though he couldn't wait to hear what she'd say next.

Maybe tonight, she'd finally kiss him. She felt like she'd been waiting forever.

The excitement of the almost-kiss earlier,

when he'd leaned in and his dark eyes went even darker had nearly convinced her not to ask him about being sentenced to work at the shack. But she'd known she'd regret the kiss if she couldn't live with whatever he'd done to earn the punishment.

Another part of her *knew* in a non-psychic way that she could trust him. That certainty inside her had made her come to the shack tonight and send Courtney away. Woman's intuition? Or just feeling so close to him, as though she knew him from long ago, not just three days. Maybe in another life.

"Did your friend Daisy get scared in the shack?" Paul asked as he started the truck.

"Yeah, but she's tough for eight."

"Eight?"

Mariah heard the surprise in his voice. "She's had some health problems. Courtney didn't go into it. I think the family's trying to put it behind them like it never happened, but you can't just make that stuff disappear."

He adjusted a vent on the dashboard to blow warm air toward her. The night had turned from chilly to downright cold. "I'm glad she liked the shack. She really likes you."

"Maybe it's because of all the time in the hospital or maybe because she's been at death's door, but Courtney says if Daisy likes you, she gives you her whole heart. And she always gives her honest opinion, like she knows there's not enough time in this world to BS." It hurt to think she might have never met her little friend. "I like kids in general, but Daisy's special."

"It shows. That you like kids, I mean. Have you thought about teaching elementary school?"

She looked out into the dark at the silent shack. "Yeah, I have, but it wouldn't be history. And you met my dad. He'd say it's no better than babysitting."

"Oh man," Paul said on a chuckle. "He should talk to my sister-in-law's cousin Rachel. She's a teacher in Longmont and tutored me and Anita."

Mariah laughed. "Another relative? Does your sister-in-law know everyone?"

He nodded. "Rachel would set him straight. And get him to sponsor events at the school."

Mariah stuck out her hand. "Buddy, you've got a bet."

He raised a brow, flicking his gaze at her hand. "I can think of a better way to seal a bet."

He leaned toward her and she met him halfway, her heart racing.

His warmth surrounded her just as his arms pulled her close and their lips met.

She'd waited forever for his kiss, and she wanted to devour him. To climb inside him and make him a part of her. The gentleness of his kiss surprised her, and at first, she was a little frustrated. *Get on with it*, she wanted to scream, and struggled to find some patience. Maybe guys moved slower in Montana.

But once she put aside her thoughts, she felt. Simply felt. His warm breath against her cheek. The gentle but firm pressure of his lips. The scent of the outdoors on him. The warmth of his skin.

His mouth moved against hers, and she just melted. Who wanted to go fast? She'd have missed the wonder and excitement tingling inside her body. Rushing, she would have failed to notice the passion he held in check. She wanted to say *let go*, but she knew that time would come. They'd be in a hurry someday. They'd touch and fumble at each other's clothes. Someday. For now, this kiss, with this guy, on this night was perfection.

Sealing a bet had never been sweeter.

"What will I win?" she whispered against his lips, thinking of what she'd wager, of what she'd offer and be glad to pay.

He kissed her again. "Ice cream."

Surprised, she had to pull back, unable to kiss him while laughing. Paul had no problem with the move, pursuing her with quick kisses on her face. She couldn't stop giggling, giddy with happiness.

"What's so funny?" he asked as he peppered her cheekbones with kisses.

"I was expecting something else."

"Okay, double scoop then."

"You're on."

With a smile, he turned and put the truck in reverse. She glared at the gear shift keeping her from scooting closer and snuggling against Paul.

"Why don't you drive an automatic?"

His teeth gleamed in the dashboard lights. "A real man can handle his stick."

She blinked, taken off guard.

"Oh, crap," Paul said. "I'm sorry. I shouldn't have—"

Mariah burst out laughing. "It's okay. I'm just surprised."

"No, no. I shouldn't have said it." He ran a hand into his hair. "It's not right to talk like that with you."

"Paul, it's okay. I've heard worse. I've *said* worse."

He glanced at her. "Really?"

"I'm not made of sugar." She waited a beat then when he made no response, continued the thought. "I won't melt in the rain."

He smiled. "You don't talk like anyone around here, but I get it."

"On a more serious note," she said as she settled back into her seat. "We're not making any progress on finding out what happened to Beezer's fortune. We might need to pull in my mom after all."

"I thought you wanted to keep her out of it."

Mariah sighed. "I do, and I would if we were close to having the smallest hint, but we can't even find a record of his name."

"If you're not okay with asking your mom, we can keep looking. The shack is open for another week and won't be torn down until a couple days after that."

"Oh," she groaned. "I forgot about it being razed." She gave him directions to Courtney's before continuing. "My mom's awesome and I love to watch her work. Work her magic, I mean. She's so... I don't know. Natural?"

"I've never been to a séance. What's it like?"

"Mom probably won't do a séance like you see on TV. She has in the past, but it's not necessary in order to communicate. She gets better results just opening up to the spirit."

"Cool. Can't wait to see it." He glanced at her. "Unless I shouldn't?"

"No, it's all good. Mom will tell you what to do."

"I have the keys, and the shack is closed during the day. Is she working tomorrow? Or," he said, "if she can't manage the daytime, we can do it after closing. Would that be a better time for the ghost to come out?"

"I don't know if it matters. People see apparitions at all times of the day. I'll ask Mom what's best and when she's available." Mariah had to steady her breathing. This had snowballed from a random idea of "maybe" to a plan of action in a few sentences.

But she'd be seeing Paul tomorrow, so that made it all worthwhile.

***

Paul sat down with Mike and Grace at the dining room table. Anita had gone to the next town over to the movies, which gave them time to talk. They'd had fried chicken for dinner, Mike's favorite, which should put him in a good mood. Paul needed all the advantage he could get, since Mike wouldn't like what Paul had to say.

"What's going on?" Mike sat tense, in full father-role-model mode. As the oldest, Mike had raised his six younger siblings since he was seventeen when their parents died. Paul didn't agree with every decision Mike had made, and the past few years had been tough, but now Paul had nothing but respect and love for his brother.

Which only made this conversation harder.

"I've come to a decision about the future. I'm going to be a mechanic. I know it's not what you want for me, Mike. You want better, or what you think is a better life."

His brother nodded.

"But see, this is *my* idea of a better life. This fits me. When I research different jobs, looking for what I want to do for the next sixty years, this just feels right." He took a breath. "I'm sorry. I know you're disappointed, but it's what I want."

Mike gave a frustrated growl. "You have so much potential."

"Maybe." Paul shrugged. "But this is what I'd be happy doing. And you've always wanted us to be happy, right?"

Grace bit back a smile and put her hand on Mike's where it lay fisted on the table. "You do always say that."

"He doesn't need any help," Mike grumbled. "He's strong headed enough."

"I wonder where he learned that." She

fluttered her eyelashes at Mike.

"Don't be cute." But his brother's shoulders looked less tense. Grace had that effect on Mike. They were perfect together. She could tease him out of being so serious and he balanced her artistic sometimes flighty nature.

Paul jumped on the opportunity. "I want to figure out a way to go to Billings next semester. If we can find a way to pay for it. You know what I've saved, and it's not much. But I'll learn more at mechanic school than I can at Clem's Garage."

"Are you thinking of a bank loan?" Mike asked.

"We can co-sign for you," Grace said. "Or I can ask my broker to sell a painting at a discount to get you started."

Paul's chest filled with gratitude. She'd sold some of her paintings the year before when she went on the run, but he hated to ask her to do it for him. "Thank you. That means a lot. I hope it doesn't come to that, though."

She shrugged. "We're family."

Paul smiled. He hadn't been kidding when he'd told Mariah of the importance of family. "I talked to Clem at the garage. He can't sponsor me, but he's checking with other garages that might pay for my schooling. In return, I'd work for them during school breaks, then for a period after I graduate, at a lower pay rate."

"Hopefully you can stay close," Grace said.

"Clem said he'd write a referral for me with the college if they have scholarships. I want you to have money for Anita next year and to finish paying for Robby."

"I'm sure we're poor enough to qualify for something," Mike said.

Grace nodded. "And having two kids in college works in our favor."

Mike cocked an eyebrow. "Does this girl you met have anything to do with your decision?"

"Meeting Mariah definitely started me thinking about the future. I need to get off my butt and get more serious about earning money. Just get serious in general."

"I need to thank her for that, at least." Mike gave a slight smile.

"Hey, I wanted to do this before I even met her. I agreed to take an online class, remember?

This is simply an adjustment to that plan." Paul looked at Grace. He hadn't brought a girl home, ever. "Is there a time we can have her out for dinner? I brought her out riding a couple of days ago, but I want everyone to meet her."

"Definitely. I'd love that. Anytime."

"Maybe when the haunted shack closes?"

"Anytime," Grace repeated. "We'll make it happen."

"How are you going to keep seeing her if you're off at school? Oh, wait." Mike shook his head. "Don't tell me. I think I know."

Paul grinned. "Mariah's going to Billings next semester too. Different degree, but on the same campus."

"Amazing coincidence," Mike said.

The next afternoon worked better for a séance for Mrs. Davis's schedule, or in her words, "the sooner the better." The Spirit might come forward at any time, although night was traditional and could be more successful. If the daytime attempt failed, she'd try again later in the week after the shack closed for the evening.

If Paul were being honest, which he definitely was not, he'd admit to being a little spooked at the idea. He didn't like the unknown or messing with the supernatural. Just in case. Conducting the séance while the townsfolk were busy in their day jobs and no one was on-site meant fewer people might take notice. And the daytime wasn't as eerie. Being at the shack at night hadn't bothered him, but purposely conjuring a ghost put a different spin on things.

While Mrs. Davis prepared herself in her car, something Mariah called "opening and protecting," they set up the room. He moved a table to the middle of the first room where the tours entered and put three folding chairs around it that he and Mariah had picked up from her friend Courtney. Just as her mom walked inside, Mariah covered the table with a cloth from her mom's box of supplies.

"What's that for?" Paul asked.

"To keep us from getting splinters," Mariah said.

He laughed. Despite the hour and brightness outside, Mariah lit a white candle. Otherwise, the setup looked pretty ordinary to him. "Anything else, Mrs. Davis?"

"Yes, you can call me Tess."

He bit back a smile. He'd looked up the song that inspired Mariah's name. "Tess" was what the singer called the rain. And "Joe" was fire, which, having met Mariah's dad, Paul could totally see. It sure must be interesting when the Davis family got riled. Rain and wind and fire, all in one room.

No, wait. He didn't believe in this stuff. The parents' names were coincidence, and they'd intentionally named Mariah to go with the song. Paul wasn't about to get carried away by the magic nonsense. He glanced at Mariah taking a seat by her mom and had to admit, he just might let himself get carried away with a certain girl.

"So we're ready?" he asked, just stopping himself from rubbing damp palms on his jeans as he pulled his chair up to the table.

"It'll be fine, Paul," call-me-Tess said. "I'm a practicing psychic medium, or I was, back in Illinois, and we're very protective of those present with us."

She was so open with him, it made him feel guilty. "I'm not sure I believe," he blurt out in the need to be equally truthful. "I can wait outside if that would help. In case the ghost won't show because I'm here, a skeptic."

"You don't have to believe. Just don't make my daughter feel bad about her abilities."

Mariah rolled her eyes. "Mom."

Abilities? Had she mentioned anything about this? "What can she do?" he asked Tess.

"I'm sitting right here," Mariah said.

"I wasn't sure you'd tell me," Paul said. "You haven't yet."

"And that would be her decision," her mother said.

Mariah sighed. "I have some sight or maybe just some concentrated intuition, and I really can conjure the wind."

Conjure the wind?

"The first time we were positive she did it, she was only three. And, Paul" —a beaming Tess put a hand on his forearm— "she doesn't usually tell anyone. She must be very comfortable with you."

Before he could reply, if he could have thought of the right thing to say, Tess closed her eyes and bowed her head.

He glanced at Mariah, trying to keep an open mind. He didn't want to push her away, but he'd never heard of anything like it. "Any other abilities?" he whispered to Mariah. She just smiled.

The one fat candle glowed in the middle of the table, leaving the rest of the room in shadows. The only window, situated near the door, had been covered with newspaper decades ago. Chill breezes had found their way into the usually stifling cabin.

Paul looked at Mariah, bringer of wind. No, he didn't believe in that stuff. In October, the wind blew and made things cold. The electronics which usually warmed the building were turned off. With only three people present, there was less body heat than when they had tours. Nothing supernatural was going on here.

He shouldn't let himself get carried away with all these mystical ideas. He didn't understand Mariah's conviction, but he believed that she believed.

"Please turn off your cell phones," Tess said.

Paul checked his again then whispered, "Done. Nothing electric has power to it since I didn't turn on the generator."

A moment of silence followed. His body went tight with anticipation.

"We're here to talk to Beezer, a miner, who died in this cabin," Tess said in a calm voice. She held her hands at shoulder level in mid-air, palms up. "If Beezer is here, please make your presence known."

They waited in silence. Tension lay heavy as a brick across Paul's shoulders. Mariah and Tess sat unperturbed, but he worried about what he could do to protect them if something bad came forward.

Not that he believed it would.

"We've heard," Tess continued, "you had a fortune in gold. That you worked hard in the mines for this gold. Can you give us a sign to confirm that?"

They waited. Nothing.

"We believe you died of an illness in this

cabin. Can you make a noise or give us any sign to confirm that?"

Nothing.

"Is your name Raines?" After a second, Tess nodded. "There's a stirring."

"I feel it," Mariah said.

Paul felt like a lump. He didn't sense anything unusual.

Tess asked questions, offered ideas to appease Beezer's spirit, and then opened the conversation to anyone who might be present that knew the miner, but Beezer and his friends didn't show.

She looked at Paul and shrugged. "I'm sorry. This happens sometimes. If the Spirit isn't willing, there's nothing we can do."

Mariah patted her arm, much like Tess did to others. "It's okay, Mom. I felt him too." She turned to Paul. "I'm sensitive, but I don't communicate. I'm not a medium."

"Well, you tried, Tess," was all he could think to say. He hadn't expected anything else so his disappointment was for Mariah and Tess. It might have been cool to make contact, though.

"There is a presence," Tess said. "It doesn't want to talk with us, but I can feel it. I'd like to come back in a few nights when we learn more information. See if I can draw it forward."

Mariah laughed. "Learn more information? Are you in on the hunt now?"

"I'm an excellent researcher. You'd be smart to take advantage of that."

They helped her gather her things, including the candle. When Paul returned from taking the box to her car, she hugged them both. "You should be okay. This presence isn't here to hurt either one of you or anyone on the tour."

Paul blinked as she left. He tried to adjust back to normal, flipping on the battery-operated miner's lantern and closing the door so no one would come to see why it stood open. The lantern served as decoration but could also be used in an emergency if the electricity failed during a tour. "So there's really a ghost here?"

Mariah leaned against the table. "There is if Mom says so, and I felt something. I wish Beezer had come forward and answered our questions."

Paul made an effort to stop looking over his

shoulder at the nothingness around the room. "Who do you think is here?"

"Hard to say. How many people have lived, or died, on this land since humans first inhabited this area?"

He chuckled. "Good point. Maybe it's Beezer's friend, and he's too ashamed of having stolen Beezer's gold to face your mom."

"Andy?"

Lights blasted on in the next room, followed by thunder. Paul and Mariah both spun toward the far room with the lightning effect. His heart nearly burst from his chest in fright. Chills ran down his skin. At least he hadn't screamed.

"What was that?" Mariah croaked, voice heavy with fear.

"It sounded like the lightning storm." Paul's body had turned clammy with cold sweat. "But it couldn't be. The generator's off so it doesn't have any power."

"It might have power," she whispered. "Just not from the generator."

In slow motion, they pivoted as one to look behind them.

A figure shimmered not ten feet away from Paul near the electronics closet. Clear as day, he thought, feeling a little light-headed. He could see right through the guy.

The copper taste of fear filled Paul's mouth as he stepped closer to protect Mariah, not sure how to combat it if it attacked them. A ghost, *a freaking ghost,* stood directly in front of him. Paul couldn't believe it. Except, he couldn't un-see the man either, so it must be real on some level.

The figure looked too well-dressed to be a miner. His clothing seemed old-fashioned, like something a man wore back in London in those movies Grace liked to watch. Or maybe this had been the fashion in the late 1800s back East in America. A black jacket and a vest covered a white buttoned shirt with a frilly front. Black slacks were tucked into tall field boots, a little too dressy for working a ranch and definitely not sturdy enough for mining. A top hat, like Abe Lincoln's only shorter, dangled from his fingers. Was this what Beezer wore before he came out West to mine for gold?

Or could it be Andy? Everyone believed he'd been a farmer who'd gotten gold fever, but perhaps he'd been a city fellow. Paul rejected that idea. Andy was supposed to have been even poorer and just as worn down as Beezer.

Only seconds had passed as Paul took in the sight, though it seemed longer. He touched Mariah's arm to draw her attention to the apparition, but she was already staring at the ghost, her eyes huge. At least she saw it too.

"Beezer?" she whispered. Then after a moment when the ghost didn't move, "Are you from Kansas too, like your friend?"

The ghost vanished and the lantern flicked off. Once his vision adjusted to the dark, Paul glanced around, making sure the spirit had gone and not just moved somewhere else—especially behind them. Hating to leave Mariah's side, Paul edged to the left, gaze glued to the spot the ghost had stood. Opening the outside door to let in light, he saw no one but Mariah in the room.

"Is he gone?" he asked.

"I think so."

Their gazes darted around the room. Paul

wanted to laugh it off in what he acknowledged as a nervous reaction. He blew out his breath. "Okay, I'm a believer."

She giggled.

"Are you okay?"

"Yeah." She sank against the table again. "I feel like I've run a marathon though."

"Me too." He took a chair at her side, then after a moment pulled her onto his lap. Maybe it was too soon to be this intimate but screw it. He needed the comfort of her close to him. The solid presence of another human. The reality of being alive.

"It's like this sometimes," she said. "Draining. The spirit needs to draw energy from somewhere or someone. In this case, us. He made the light turn on and then the lantern go out, and the storm effect flickering was him too. It took a lot of energy for him to materialize."

They glanced to where he'd stood. A small piece of light brown paper lay on the floor, its ragged edges indicating it had been torn from a larger piece of paper.

"Was that there before?" she asked, gaze

transfixed.

Paul shook his head, mouth dry. Goosebumps crawled over his skin.

She blew out a breath. "Wow. It took a lot of energy for him to leave that."

They stared at it.

"Do you think it has anything written on it?" he asked.

She strained to see from where she sat. "Can't tell."

He didn't want to get closer to it, but curiosity nudged him.

"Mom's going to be upset to have missed this."

"Who's going to touch *that*?" Paul said on a laugh. He knew he would. In a second. He needed to take a breath to calm his heartbeat. And maybe a prayer wouldn't hurt.

Okay, time to suck it up. He gave Mariah a quick hard hug then set her to her feet. Stepping toward the paper, he kept his gaze glued to it, like it might fly at him or something. Who knew what to expect now? He sure as hell had no idea. His world had been viciously rocked in the past few moments.

The paper didn't attack him. Picking it up, he read it, passing the thick stationery paper between his fingers. It looked old-fashioned, but what did he know about paper textures from back then or how they aged?

"What's it say?" Mariah asked.

He handed it to her.

She took it, fingers trembling.

Max

Just one word, creating more questions. The most obvious one being the one Mariah spoke for both of them:

"Who's Max?"

CHAPTER FIVE

"DO YOU HAVE time to do this?" Mariah asked as they rushed into her house to use the computer. The library might have been faster, but home was closer. And Mom was working, so searching on the library computers would have created questions. They wanted to do this themselves since Max hadn't appeared until they were alone. But she didn't want to tell Mom that and hurt her feelings.

Paul laughed. "I'll make time."

She understood his excitement. She'd felt the same reckless exuberance the first time Mom had allowed her to meet a spirit. Like, if ghosts were possible, anything was.

They tore through the house, knowing Mom had gone to work and Dad would be out supervising reconstruction of the stables.

Glasses of water revived them as the Internet icon spun. Paul hadn't let go of her hand during the drive and held it now. She didn't mind one bit. Maybe he needed human contact after encountering the supernatural, but she chose to believe he was also attracted to her. Time would tell.

"Do you think the ghost was Beezer before he came here?" Paul asked. "He left us a name, probably his son's, right? Thinking we could get the gold to him?"

Mariah shook her head. "I don't know. Even before we saw the paper, I sensed it wasn't Beezer. He felt younger and almost like a foreigner. Not from outside the U.S., but a stranger in a strange land kind of thing."

"Which would describe everyone who came West back then."

"True, but I don't think this ghost ever worked out here."

"Again, that could be Beezer before he got to Montana." Paul took a gulp of water. "So why do you think it's not him?"

"Because this guy, this ghost, is looking for something or someone specific."

Paul eyed her. Now that he couldn't deny the supernatural existed, he had to believe in her powers too. He might have to experience the wind thing before he bought in to it, but he totally accepted that Mariah could sense more in the world than he knew.

"There it goes." She typed in "RAINES, MAX, ANDY, KANSAS" this time. "I added Kansas because the ghost blew out our light when I asked if he was from there. I don't know if that meant yes or no, but it got a response, so it's worth a try."

"You're good at this."

"Years of brainstorming with Mom."

"Or your second sight?" Paul turned her chin so she'd look at him. "Why didn't you tell me? You trusted me with knowing about your mom's abilities."

Mariah shrugged, uncomfortable to have been caught. Not disclosing the truth felt like she'd outright lied. "I wanted to ease into telling you. See if you liked me first."

"Oh, sugar," he said in a low tone, laced with a smile, "I definitely like you." He leaned in and touched his lips to hers in a kiss that lingered and stirred her with a mix of joy and lust. Joy because she definitely liked him too, although it had happened so fast she should mistrust it. She should slow down but didn't want to. Lust because this was Paul, who looked like dark temptation but acted like an angel with her.

He drew back and took a breath. "When this job at the shack is over, we'll have more time together. But when they close the shack to tours after the first weekend in November, they're going to tear it down. We don't have much time."

Did she say he was an angel? He was frustration personified. An empty house and newly admitted feelings equaled a make-out session in her book. Nevertheless, she couldn't argue. They'd be distracted. This wasn't the time. Ugh. "You're right."

She turned to the screen and found a few links that looked vague, some more promising and then—

"Hey. What about this one?" Paul pointed to

the screen and she clicked on an article from a Kansas paper. They followed that link to a genealogy site. A lawyer from Kansas had set up the Raines Charitable Fund at an orphanage in his town. Mariah skimmed the article about the orphanage and how many children had passed through its doors. The Raines Fund had been responsible for providing a home for and feeding hundreds of children.

The article said the lawyer couldn't find a Raines family "back East," with no further information about them or their whereabouts. Andy told him the Raines family was wealthy but that Beezer wanted his child to be free of their control.

"Look," Paul said. "See the part about why the lawyer set up the charity?"

She jumped to read where he pointed. A bedraggled man had shown up at his law office, coughing and near to dying with consumption.

"'The lawyer wore a handkerchief over his nose and mouth while dealing with the man,'" Paul read. "Huh. He probably looked like a stagecoach robber to Andy."

"Probably. But he seems to have been honest. He set up the fund and oversaw it while he lived."

"Does it say why he didn't send it to Beezer's kid, who I still think is named Max?"

Mariah skimmed it then said, "Looks like Andy was so sick he forgot where Beezer was from. Or the lawyer didn't look very hard." She sat back and smiled. "At least Andy tried to get the money to Beezer's child. Sounds like it was a lot, if it took care of that many orphans for so long. Andy had to have been a good friend and an honest man to avoid temptation."

"The lawyer too."

"No one in Little Tree knew if Andy had betrayed his friend or not. He did leave town with the gold, and nobody knew if Beezer's name was Raines to check on it further. Or like the lawyer, even where to check for a Raines family."

Paul leaned close to the screen. "Does it say what Beezer's name was?"

She read until she found it. "Benjamin Zachariah Raines."

"BZR? Come on. That's too easy."

Mariah shrugged. "He could have had a monogram on something. A suitcase or a handkerchief even. The people out here saw it and 'Beezer' was born."

"I can see that." Paul leaned back in the chair. "And his son Max would never have heard him referred to as Beezer, so Max didn't answer when your mom asked."

"Right." Mariah blinked away the tears in her eyes. "We'll have to tell him."

"Tell who what?" her dad's voice boomed out from the doorway.

Paul swung around in the chair to see her parents standing just inside the room.

"What's going on?" her dad demanded. "If you think you're eloping with my daughter, forget about it."

"Dad! Oh my God. I can't believe you just said that. Where did that even come from?" She turned to Paul, red-faced. "I'm so sorry."

Paul forced down his anger and stared Joe straight in the eye. "It'd be my honor to call her my girlfriend, sir, but it's a little early to talk about marriage."

"That Randy kid warned me you'd be on the lookout, trying to take advantage of the setup here."

"That's crazy," Mariah said. "Why would you even listen to that moron?"

"The setup here?" Paul nearly laughed except for feeling sick to his stomach at the man's dislike of him. "I'd say you have a ways to go before you tempt me. You might have money, but my brother's ranch is already successful. I have an 'in' there, so you're safe. I won't be asking you for a job."

"You won't be getting anything from me, including my daughter."

Mariah covered her face with both hands and moaned. "Jesus God."

"Joe, calm down," Tess said.

"Our future plans, sir, will be up to Mariah. A lot of things should be her choice."

Joe took a step back. "What's that supposed to mean?"

"Paul, stop," Mariah said.

"No, I'm sorry. Your dad needs to hear this." Paul stood, a little shaky inside but determined to stand up for her. Hopefully defending her to her dad wouldn't turn Mariah against him. He'd gone through this same argument when Mike tried to decide his future. "I've done some things I'm not proud of, but I'd never do anything to hurt Mariah. She can make decisions for herself."

"I'm her father."

"Yes, sir, and you both raised her to be strong and have her own opinions." Paul smiled. "As I've found out in only a few days of knowing her. If she wants to teach little kids or be a CPA or fly a broom, you should let her."

Joe's jaw went slack with surprise. "A broom? You told him?"

Tess stepped over and put a soothing hand on his arm. "Paul's very open-minded. I like him."

Mariah looked at her mother. "We found him, Mom. The spirit. Max, I think. And we have a message for him."

"Then go," Tess said.

They pushed past Joe, who didn't try to stop them, but halfway out of the house, Mariah ran back and planted a kiss on her dad's cheek. "I'll be back in a few hours."

***

They sped to the haunted house and ran in, closing the door. Paul turned on the lantern. At the last minute, he wondered if he should have brought new batteries but the bulb inside lit.

"I've never done this," Mariah said, shaking the tension out of her hands. "I've watched Mom and I've had sensations when spirits were present, but Max was the first full-bodied apparition I've seen."

"You can do it," Paul assured her. "He responded to you before when you talked about Andy. He's probably here because he heard stories about his dad's fortune. Andy never brought him the gold, so he wants answers."

"What if he doesn't show himself? How will we know he heard the message?"

"If he doesn't show or give us a sign, we'll have your mom come and tell him."

"Okay, good plan. Nothing to lose if I mess it up." She took a deep breath and composed herself through a simple meditative cleansing mantra. She sensed things better or used her "second sight" as her dad called it, more clearly when she was calm. Mom had shown her how to settle her mind years ago when Mariah had stirred the wind too often with her emotions.

"Max," she called in the firm, even voice her mom often used, "we did some research into your father's past. Your dad wanted you to have his money. Unfortunately, his gold never arrived because his friend, Andy, died on the way to give it to you. But Andy tried. He didn't betray your father."

"Tell him," Paul whispered, "that Andy got sick taking care of Beezer."

"Did you hear that, Max? They had what was called consumption in your time and I think we call it tuberculosis. Your father probably became sick while mining."

She paused and looked at Paul, who nodded for her to continue.

"His work wasn't all for nothing. Your dad's fortune provided for other children in an orphanage. He wound up doing good in the world, although not the way he wanted. He wanted you to inherit. He wanted you to be independent of your family."

Max's head and torso shimmered into view. He smiled, gave a nod and disappeared.

Paul hugged Mariah, who was content to be quiet in the shared moment. After a few minutes, he kissed her cheek. "You did it."

She nodded.

"You know, I'm starting to wonder if you did something witchy to me." When she frowned, he continued. "Like maybe you conjured the wind to sweep me off my feet."

Mariah laughed. "Is that how it happened?"

"That's the result anyway. I'm pretty much a goner for you."

She stood on tiptoe and hooked her arms around his neck. "It's entirely mutual."

He kissed her lightly then said, "Let me get you back home before your dad sends a posse after me."

Disappointment dragged at her stomach. "We don't have to go right now."

"Yeah, we do. Face it, your dad doesn't like me."

"He just doesn't know you yet."

"No, he's right. I've done things I'm not proud of. I party too much, or I used to, and that always involved drinking."

"Everyone does."

"No, Mariah, it's not that simple. I want to be better."

"I'm not perfect either."

"I think you are. Or if you're not, you're pretty darn close."

"That's a lot to live up to."

"Just be yourself. That's enough for me."

Her insides turned to mush and she melted into his arms. Her parents' expectations for her were lovingly meant but only compounded the pressure she felt trying to figure out what she wanted to do for the rest of her life. Just being herself sounded like heaven.

She argued her case to stay at the shack, but despite her trying to coerce him with kisses until her knees went weak, Paul stood firm. "Your dad thinks I'm introducing you to another definition of 'shacking up.'"

Shaking her head, Mariah let him lead her outside. With a last look at the old cabin, she said a silent goodbye to Max, Beezer, and Andy. Just in case.

As they neared home, she spotted Dad at the door wearing a frown.

"Here we go," Paul said.

"It'll be all right. Dad went a little crazy there for a minute, thinking we were going to, you know, get married." She gave a laugh to show she thought it was crazy too. "We haven't even known each other a week."

"So once we've known each other longer?" Paul teased. "Is that a proposal?"

She laughed and climbed from the truck. "We'll see."

Dad scowled at them but he invited Paul in for dessert. No doubt Mom's influence at work. "Well then, let's hear about your ghost."

Mariah beamed, blinking back sudden tears. "Daddy."

He harrumphed. "Not that I believe in such things, but I've lived with your mother long enough to... wonder."

Mom's eyes went wide. "That's the most positive thing you've ever said about our abilities. There's hope for you yet, Joe."

Mariah set dessert plates and forks on the table and poured everyone iced tea.

"We have milk too." Mom set a golden crusted dessert on the table. "Both go with apple pie."

"That's my favorite dessert," Paul said.

Mom just smiled at him. Paul nodded in understanding.

Her mom had not only known his favorite pie and made it for him, but she'd also known he'd be present to enjoy it at some time this week. He'd have to get used to this kind of thing, Mariah thought.

"First," she said, feeling a little jittery inside, "before we tell you about the ghost at the shack, I need to say this. I want to take some classes in education. See if I like it."

Dad gave a hard scowl and she almost took a step back. She could never fear him, but she hated to disappoint him.

"Don't you think she'd be a good teacher?" Paul challenged.

"Of course I do," Dad protested, the angry frown mark between his eyes returning. "She'll be great at whatever she sets her mind to do." He paused, his wide eyes looking trapped. "No, wait. I meant—"

But everyone else just laughed.

"Don't worry about her living away from home, sir," Paul said. "I'm going to be in Billings next semester too. I'll watch out for her."

Mariah's heart leapt. They'd have lots of time together between now and January when term started, and they wouldn't have to be apart while she went to college.

"What a coincidence," Dad muttered.

Mariah knew her dad and Paul would eventually come to an understanding and they'd wind up friends. At least she hoped so.

Paul had almost proposed the first time they'd met. She'd almost proposed today. Mariah had a feeling there'd be nothing "almost" about the next time.

She only wondered which one of them would pop the question.

****

For information on my upcoming books and the occasional goodie, please join my newsletter (type eepurl.com/dlq1dP into your browser). Or you can visit my website at megankellybooks.com and sign up there.

If you have a minute, I'd appreciate a short review wherever you bought this book or on a reader or retailer site. Thanks for reading.

"A Risky Proposal" a short story featured in *Wild Deadwood Tales*, is available free when you sign up for my newsletter. The action takes place before *Coming Home* (book 4) but you can enjoy it anytime as a stand-alone.

Author's Note

I usually say "writing this book has been a labor of love," but actually, this one was just plain fun. Learning more about Paul made my heart happy, as he's a difficult character. I wanted to see him progress down the rocky road he's chosen and maybe start on a smoother path. I've never featured such a young heroine, and I'm pleased with who Mariah turned out to be. She surprised and amused me; I hope you liked her too.

Forming the Common Elements Romance Project in 2019, approximately seventy authors chose to write five items into their books: a person/animal named Max, a lightning storm, lost keys, a stack of books, and a "haunted" house. How to weave in these Elements came to me while I was finishing *Baby Makes Three* and this story percolated. That tends to be the pattern with my writing—the next romance story starts butting its head against my fingers like a playful kitten while I try to concentrate on the work in progress. I wouldn't want it any other way! Maybe because Halloween is my second-favorite holiday, the rest of Paul's story just fell into place.

Thank you for reading my books. If you enjoyed this story, I'd appreciate you leaving a review at your favorite retailer. Reviews help authors in so many ways. Other readers also rely on your review to help them find a story (like mine, hopefully) that they will enjoy. No book summary necessary. If you leave a few simple sentences and some stars, I'd be grateful.

Happy reading,
Megan

Other Books by Megan Kelly

To read more about these titles, please visit my website
megankellybooks.com.

Love in Little Tree series:
The Wedding Rescue
Runaway Bride
Baby Makes Three
Coming Home

Christmas in Stilton series:
Santa Dear
Holly & Ivey

Returning Home series
Fixer-Upper

Harlequin American Romances:
Marrying the Boss

The Fake Fiancée
The Marriage Solution
Stand-In Mom
(reprinted in No Ordinary Family)

About the Author

Megan Kelly writes heart-warming contemporary romance set in small towns. After selling four books to Harlequin, she ventured into self-publishing.

Her "Love in Little Tree" series celebrates Montana cowboys, while her other romances feature fictional Midwest towns. Quirky secondary characters might briefly steal the spotlight, but romance is always center stage.

Fortunately, she has a very supportive husband and two kids who don't remember a time when Mom didn't write. She lives in the St. Louis area, where the weather has an imagination (and sense of humor) of its own.

You can sign up for her Readers' Group newsletter at eepurl.com/dlq1Dp or on her website page at megankellybooks.com.

www.ingramcontent.com/pod-product-compliance
Lightning Source LLC
Chambersburg PA
CBHW060622130626
46555CB00002B/621